A gunshot rang out. Too close...

Landon figured the only thing that saved him and Hazeleigh was the dark.

"We have to get you out of here."

"Me?" she all but shrieked. *"Us."*

Another shot. Hazeleigh winced and grabbed on to him. Landon tried to survey where the gunfire was coming from. He'd seen a silhouette inside the house, but it couldn't be whoever was shooting at them...unless the shooter had a window open.

Possible. Far too many possibilities.

Landon stilled, pushed Hazeleigh out of his mind and listened. He blew out a slow breath, finding that old center of calm. He pushed away all the worries, concerns and possibilities, and focused on the now.

A cold ball of fear pitted in his stomach. Footsteps. Coming for them. He grabbed Hazeleigh's hand. He had to get her somewhere safe.

ONE NIGHT STANDOFF

NICOLE HELM

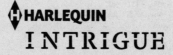

To the old men who study history and spill soup on
their keyboards.

HARLEQUIN®
INTRIGUE™

Recycling programs
for this product may
not exist in your area.

ISBN-13: 978-1-335-58247-8

One Night Standoff

Copyright © 2023 by Nicole Helm

For questions and comments about the quality of this book,
please contact us at CustomerService@Harlequin.com.

Harlequin Enterprises ULC
22 Adelaide St. West, 41st Floor
Toronto, Ontario M5H 4E3, Canada
www.Harlequin.com

Printed in U.S.A.

Nicole Helm grew up with her nose in a book and the dream of one day becoming a writer. Luckily, after a few failed career choices, she gets to follow that dream—writing down-to-earth contemporary romance and romantic suspense. From farmers to cowboys, Midwest to *the* West, Nicole writes stories about people finding themselves and finding love in the process. She lives in Missouri with her husband and two sons, and dreams of someday owning a barn.

Books by Nicole Helm

Harlequin Intrigue

Covert Cowboy Soldiers

The Lost Hart Triplet
Small Town Vanishing
One Night Standoff
Shot in the Dark

A North Star Novel Series

Summer Stalker
Shot Through the Heart
Mountainside Murder
Cowboy in the Crosshairs
Dodging Bullets in Blue Valley
Undercover Rescue

A Badlands Cops Novel

South Dakota Showdown
Covert Complication
Backcountry Escape
Isolated Threat
Badlands Beware
Close Range Christmas

Visit the Author Profile page at Harlequin.com.

CAST OF CHARACTERS

Hazeleigh Hart—Historical research assistant who's just found her boss murdered, triplet to Zara, living at the small cabin on the now-Thompson property. Sometimes has "premonitions." She knows she's going to be accused of Mr. Field's murder and doesn't want to go to the police.

Landon Thompson—One of six ex-military men now running a ranch. Accidentally catches Hazeleigh running away and becomes determined to help prove Hazeleigh isn't a murderer, but falls for her as she's thrust into more and more danger.

Mr. Field—Eccentric older man who runs the historical fort and researches an old bank robbery. Hazeleigh's murdered boss whose body she finds.

Zara Hart—Hazeleigh's triplet, ranch hand for the Thompsons and now living at the main house on the Thompson property with Jake Thompson.

Jake Thompson—One of the ex-military, now-ranching Thompson brothers. Living with Zara at the main house.

Brody, Henry and Dunne Thompson—The rest of the Thompson brothers, all ex-military and working the ranch.

Kate Phillips—Hazeleigh's childhood friend who also works at the fort and is dating Brody.

Chapter One

It couldn't be happening again.

Hazeleigh Hart stood in the doorway to her boss's office and was sure she was in the midst of a nightmare.

There was blood. So much—too much—blood.

Mr. Field was most decidedly dead.

There was grief and denial. Emotions battered Hazeleigh, but the one that finally made her move was fear.

This was not the first dead body she'd uncovered in the past year. The last time it happened, the police had been sure she'd had something to do with the murder, before her sister had helped clear her.

Murder. Who would want to kill poor old Mr. Field, an eccentric man who paid for her to do research, and to organize his own, about a supposed bank robbery in Wilde back in the 1800s?

But it didn't matter who. It didn't matter how or when. It only mattered that she was alive, and the only one standing here looking at his dead body. He had to have been murdered. There was no other explanation for all that blood.

She hadn't had a bad feeling this time—like last

year, when her sister Zara had accidentally dug up
their other sister's body. No, Mr. Field's lifeless body—
slumped over his work in his office—was a complete
and utter surprise.

Would anyone believe it?

No.

Her whole life she'd been plagued by bad premonitions, so to speak, but they were neither consistent nor
always correct, which meant no one ever believed her.
They didn't believe her if she said something bad was
going to happen before it did, and they didn't believe
her when she said she hadn't felt anything before something bad *had* happened either.

Except Zara. Sometimes. Her living sister was the
only person who ever believed her, but Hazeleigh knew
even if Zara trusted her innocence—and she would,
because Zara always believed her to be innocent—
she wouldn't be able to do anything about how bad it
looked.

No one would.

Slowly, Hazeleigh backed out of the office. Her
stomach was queasy, and her eyes burned with tears.
Mr. Field was a sweet old man. He wouldn't hurt anyone. The harshest thing she'd ever heard him say was
"fiddlesticks" when he spilled soup on his keyboard.

She'd had to type all his emails for him while he
waited for it to be fixed—he hadn't wanted the expense of buying a new one, though he could have af-
forded it easily.

A sob rose in her throat, and she managed to turn
away from the body.

She would have to go away. Away from here. The

death. The blood. Away from poor Mr. Field and all his research. Away from Wilde, Wyoming—the only place she'd ever really been.

She would have to disappear.

She had been to jail. Well, a holding cell. It wasn't the end of the world, but… She felt something *wrong* deep inside of her. Consistent or not, *right* or not, she just *knew* letting the police investigate her would end badly for her.

She had to disappear. She walked out of the fort— the historic building where Mr. Field had his office—to her car in the parking lot. She began to drive to the Hart Ranch, eyes always in the rearview mirror, certain sirens and lights would appear behind her at any moment.

She would go to her cabin, pack up her things and start driving. It didn't matter where she ended up. She just had to escape.

Dimly, in the back of her mind, Hazeleigh understood this was blind panic. She couldn't really disappear. She needed time to think. To settle and *think*.

She parked in front of her cabin. It wasn't safe here. They'd come for her here. She couldn't go to Zara. Zara would call Thomas, their cousin, who was a police officer. Zara would think he could help.

But Hazeleigh wouldn't get her sister and cousin wrapped up in this. Or Jake, one of the Thompson brothers who'd been shot trying to unravel the whole mystery revolving around her other sister's murder.

Jake, who she'd just gone to the jewelry store with yesterday to help pick out a ring for Zara.

It had taken some time, but Hazeleigh had finally

felt comfortable around him. He'd won her over with patience and kindness and space.

She didn't feel comfortable around men as a rule. Her father had blamed her for Amberleigh's disappearance long before the murder, and he sometimes got violent when he could hide it from Zara.

The two men she'd trusted enough to date had both turned violent in the end—Douglas had even murdered Amberleigh, thinking it was Hazeleigh.

Hazeleigh shuddered. No, she didn't trust men—at least ones who showed any interest in her.

But Mr. Field and Jake were fine. Even the Thompson brothers had gotten easier to be around. They ran the Hart Ranch now, after all. She had to be around them.

And they would all want to help. Hazeleigh knew every last one of them would try to help her. But no one would be able to prove she hadn't done it. She would end up in jail.

She couldn't. She couldn't.

Panic was its own beat inside of her now. No amount of reason could penetrate. She packed a bag.

Where are you going? Where can you go?

She surveyed the ranch outside her cabin. She wasn't safe on the ranch, but there was an awful lot of land to cover, and would they think to cover it? If she wasn't in her cabin, if she cleared everything out, wouldn't the police expect her to get as far away as possible?

She blinked at the horizon. No, she wouldn't run away. She'd hunker down right here.

And no one would ever know.

LANDON DAVIS-THOMPSON, these days, let the horse beneath him *run*.

When it came to the six men who'd come to run the Hart Ranch, Brody was more than proficient on a horse. Jake and Dunne were sidelined by injuries, but both could ride in a pinch. Henry and Cal were both too stiff and too bitter not to struggle, but they did what had to be done.

Landon, though… Landon *loved* it. He'd always loved horses. Growing up dirt-poor on a farm that barely fed its tenants, let alone its animals, he'd never dreamed this would be his life.

Even when he'd dreamed of escape, it had been to join the military. To strive for excellence there and make something out of his life—anything other than ending up like his family. His abusive father drinking himself to death, his mom grieving herself to death and all his brothers winding up in jail or six feet under.

So when Landon had been recruited by Team Breaker, a secret, elite military group meant to bring down various terrorist rings in the Middle East, he figured he'd succeeded. He'd peaked.

Then hell had broken loose, and military mistakes had turned Landon and his military brothers into direct targets. So they'd been erased. Sent to Wyoming to disappear. New identities. A new life.

Landon Davis was dead, but Landon Thompson had a future. Even if it was ranching this big spread in the middle of nowhere, Wyoming.

Landon figured he'd hate the cold northern winters, figured ranch work would be too similar to that farm life he'd grown up on, drowning in everyone else's rage and bitterness.

But as it turned out, he was happy here.

Horses. Ranching. His military brothers, this small-town life. It suited him, surprisingly enough.

Then there was Hazeleigh Hart, the pretty and far-too-skittish woman who lived in a cabin on the property the "Thompson brothers" now owned. Something about the woman had tied him up in an uncharacteristic number of knots.

Strange, considering he'd never once had a problem attracting female attention.

Except when it came to Hazeleigh. She'd never looked at him twice. Didn't even notice that he sometimes looked for too long, paid too much attention, tried a little too hard to get her to smile and stop being so nervous around him.

Which was why when he saw the telltale tangle of dark hair trailing behind a running form, pink scarf fluttering behind her, he thought maybe he'd conjured up the image in his imagination.

Because what would Hazeleigh be doing running around the far edge of the property line? Landon had spent many an afternoon running the horses out this way and never saw anyone that wasn't bovine this far back.

But it *was* someone, not a figment of his imagination, and he honestly couldn't fathom it being anyone else. "Hazeleigh?" he called out.

She looked over her shoulder, but she didn't stop running. There was terror in her eyes, which had his instincts kicking in.

He urged the horse into a run until he caught up with her, stopping the horse and swinging off in one fluid movement. He didn't grab her, like he might have with just about anyone else who appeared to be running for their life in the middle of nowhere.

He'd learned to give Hazeleigh space, so he merely placed himself in her path and held out his hands in a *stop* gesture.

She slowed, but she didn't stop, passing him on the side as she shook her head. "Please don't, Landon. Go back to the house and pretend you never saw me. You can't tell anyone you saw me."

She was breathing hard, clearly struggling. But she just kept moving, the backpack she was wearing slapping against her back. He fell into an easy jog beside her.

"Hazeleigh, I think you need to stop and take a breath and tell me what's going on."

She kept shaking her head. She was obviously running out of steam, but she kept propelling herself forward.

"I can't. I can't. You just have to go. Don't tell Zara. Don't tell anyone. Please."

When he didn't do as she asked, she finally stopped and pinned those big, brown eyes on him. "You don't understand." Her eyes filled with tears. "Mr. Field is dead."

"What?" he said, brain kicking into gear. Was this grief? *Should* he leave her alone to deal with it?

"Someone killed him." Her voice broke. "His blood…" She shook her head like she couldn't bear to say the words. "They're going to think it was me."

"I don't…" He trailed off, because her hand gripped his. Hazeleigh, who usually did everything she could to put distance between her body and his, reached out and grabbed him like he was a lifeline.

And then he heard the same thing she did.

Sirens.

Chapter Two

Already? Could it be already? It had to be. The sirens were far off, but the highway was just a few miles north. The only reason sirens would be this close, getting closer and closer, would be to make their way from town to the Hart Ranch.

"You can't tell anyone you saw me." She squeezed his hand, so big and strong even as it hung loosely in her death grip. Usually the Thompson brothers made her nervous—so big and male and...they had a kind of predatory stillness about them.

She didn't think they were bad men. Certainly not Jake, who loved her sister so much, or Brody, who'd fallen for her childhood friend, Kate. She understood they weren't mean or bad.

But there was something about their physical presence that set off that *flight* response in her, which stemmed from her own bad choices, she knew.

She was too afraid of what waited for her to be afraid of Landon and his all-encompassing *maleness* in this moment.

His left hand came up and covered her hand, which was clutching his right. He pinned her with his dark blue gaze. "Let's figure this all out. You take a deep breath and let it out," Landon instructed. He seemed so certain and so sure that she followed his orders without even thinking about it.

"Now, you found Mr. Field dead? Where? The fort?"

She nodded emphatically. "His office." His messy little office at the old historic fort he loved so much. She couldn't squeeze her eyes shut because she'd see his poor body, bloody and lifeless. So she squeezed Landon's hand. "He left me a message in the middle of the night that he'd found something, and he wanted me to come in first thing." Hazeleigh tried to blink back tears. If she'd answered, if she'd gotten there earlier, would she have been able to stop what happened?

"Now, that's evidence enough you didn't hurt him, Hazeleigh," Landon said. "Why would you think they'd try to blame you?"

She tried to pull her hand away, but Landon held firm. In the moment, she didn't fully realize that it didn't cause the panic it should have. Instead, he was something like an anchor, tethering her to reality instead of panic.

She sucked in a breath and slowly let it out again. He was right. She needed to breathe. The sirens were coming and if she was going to survive, she had to *think*.

Landon was a complication, though. She somehow needed to convince him to let her go. He couldn't get involved in this—he'd involve Zara, and Zara would want to fight for her and...

The last time that had happened, Jake had ended up shot.

Wasn't it better to take Amberleigh's original way out? Run away?

Amberleigh wound up murdered herself.

"Hazeleigh."

She blinked up at Landon. "I just…know they will." She hadn't had a feeling something was wrong, but she knew—she just *knew*—she would somehow be on the hook for this.

The sirens were closer now, likely at the front gate of the ranch. They'd go to her cabin first, or maybe the main house. Not all the way out here. She still had time.

"Please, can't you just go and pretend you never saw me?"

He frowned, which was rare. Landon was easygoing, always ready with a joke. He was the only one of the brothers who seemed genuinely cheerful. She would have called him charming, if she didn't second-guess herself when it came to charming.

"This is what we're going to do," he said, with a take-charge air that usually came from his brother Cal. His eyes scanned the horizon. He squinted and she knew he was looking at the building she'd been heading to.

"That little building out there—anyone ever use that?"

Hazeleigh shook her head. "Technically, it's on Peterson land, and mostly the last generation of Petersons left Wilde but kept the land, and let all their buildings go to rot. It was once a schoolhouse, but it's just a shack at this point." She didn't mention it had been her plan to hide there.

He nodded. "All right, let's go."

He didn't let her go, just started pulling her along. He grabbed his horse's reins and walked her alongside them.

Hazeleigh gave the horse a side-eye. Buttercup had once been hers. She'd never loved the ranch like Zara. She'd been far more interested in books and history and homemaking pursuits over cattle and crops and chores.

But Buttercup had been *hers*, and then Dad sold Hart Ranch and everything on it to the Thompson brothers, because they'd been willing to pay over market price.

It had been Zara's fast talking last fall that had convinced the Thompsons to let Zara and Hazeleigh rent their own family's cabin, and Zara stay on as a ranch hand.

Landon looked down at her, caught her staring at the horse. Hazeleigh blinked and looked straight ahead.

So her father had sold off her beloved horse. Hazeleigh got to go down to the stables and feed the mare some apple slices, her favorite, when she wanted. It wasn't as though she'd been cut off, thanks to Zara.

But Buttercup wasn't hers to ride anymore. The wildflowers that dotted the landscape weren't Hazeleigh's to pick. It seemed everywhere she turned, things were being taken away from her.

"Zara said she was yours."

Hazeleigh shrugged, trying not to be frustrated with how easily he saw through her. "More or less, but I never spent much time doing ranch work like you all. She's a ranch horse. She should be used as one."

He tied the reins to a tree at the fence line and then studied the barbed wire. "You're going to have to let me give you a hand." He found a spot where the wire was a little loose, then put his booted foot on it and used his weight to push it down. He held out his hand.

It was different this time, to take it. Because he'd offered it. Because she'd stopped panicking. She knew that this was a man who would help. The problem was she didn't want it. He was a complication she didn't have the time or wherewithal to figure out.

But he'd seen her, so she didn't have a choice. She flicked a glance at the horse. She never would have guessed Landon for the riding-by-himself type.

That was the problem. She did not trust her instincts when it came to new people, particularly men. She'd learned a very hard lesson there.

But she had to deal with the reality of the situation. He'd seen her. He would help. She had to figure out a way to use his assistance to suit her purposes.

So she had to go along with him for the moment. Until she could figure out what to do next. Until she had time to think without needing to run.

Though she was hesitating, Landon just stood there patiently. Hand outstretched, boot on the barbed wire.

Hazeleigh forced herself to move forward, to put her hand in his. He gripped it and waited for her to put her own booted foot on the wire. She lifted her skirt off the barbs with her free hand as she hopped over.

Then immediately dropped his hand.

"There we are," he said, and she knew he was trying to encourage her to keep taking the next step. Like he might encourage a horse. A skittish one at that.

He hopped over the fence in an easy movement she found oddly mesmerizing. He had a grace about him, from the horse riding to the fence hopping.

"We'll just get you hunkered down in there and then I'll get it all sorted out," he said, smiling at her reassuringly as he moved toward the old school.

"How come your brothers don't sound like you?" she asked. It was a question she'd pondered for *months*, but never felt comfortable asking. Panic had dulled her senses, or put all her anxiety somewhere else, so the question just fell out.

"I grew up in Mississippi. They didn't. Surely Zara's told you we aren't all full brothers."

Hazeleigh nodded, but something about the way he said it gave her that odd feeling she sometimes got. That something bad was coming. Something wrong.

She shook her head and looked at the little school in front of them. Mr. Field had studied this school as part of his bank-robbery research, and though it had historical importance, being on private land meant it hadn't been well cared for like the fort.

Still, did that research mean someone might look for her here? Would every place she went to hide connect to Mr. Field?

Dead Mr. Field.

She didn't have time to worry about that as Landon pushed open the door. He stepped into the musty, dim room. The desks were gone, but there was still a chalkboard on the front wall—it was cracked and probably impossible to use.

The lone window was cracked as well but not broken out, which made the interior less stuffy than it might have been.

"You weren't wrong about the shack part." He shook his head and turned to her, looking pained. "Hazeleigh, let's go on up to the house. I'm sure no one really thinks you killed Mr. Field."

"I know they do," Hazeleigh replied flatly. She just *knew*.

He studied her, then nodded. "Okay. You stay put right here, all right? I'm going to see what's what. You don't take off on me—you got that? I'll be back as soon as I know what's going on."

She chewed on her bottom lip. She wasn't sure she should trust him. "But…"

"Let's just make sure this is what you think it is. You stay put, and I won't tell the police or Zara a thing. Promise." He held out his hand again.

He said it so fiercely, so sincerely, she thought she had to believe him. And she had to promise. She reached out and shook his hand. "All right."

She'd stay put…for now.

LANDON WASN'T CONVINCED Hazeleigh would stay, but he knew he needed to prove to her that she wasn't and wouldn't be a suspect, which meant he had to get back to the main house and determine what those sirens had been about.

He didn't know who in their right mind would think Hazeleigh was guilty of *murder*, but he understood why she thought they might, since she'd been held in connection to her own sister's murder not all that long ago.

Anyone who spent more than five minutes with her would have known better, but he supposed it wasn't the job of the police to know Hazeleigh. It was to follow evidence. Hazeleigh did work closely with Mr. Field, but who would want to kill an old, eccentric man in the middle of Wyoming, anyway?

Landon rode back to the house at a gallop, only slowing Buttercup once he could view the house. No matter how much he wanted to rush, he took his time. Even if he thought Hazeleigh was overreacting, he'd promised her that he'd see what was what without giving her away. He'd keep his promise.

He stabled the horse, then forced himself to whistle as he walked toward the house.

The scene had his instincts humming and the hope he'd had that this might blow over evaporating. Zara was standing there talking to two deputies. Her hands were on her hips and she looked furious. Kate was on the porch, and she was talking to someone on the phone.

Henry was outside the little outbuilding he'd converted into his living quarters, arms crossed. "What's going on?" Landon asked as he approached.

Henry shrugged. "Not sure."

"So you're just going to stand here?"

Henry didn't respond with more than a shrug. Landon rolled his eyes and walked over to where Zara was facing off with the officers. "What's the problem?" he asked with a pleasant smile and his best casual stance.

"Mr. Field's been murdered," Zara said, and by the way she was glaring daggers at the cops, Landon had the sinking suspicion Hazeleigh was right.

Landon had to work very hard not to match Zara's antagonistic approach, but he managed to keep calm.

"We had a call," one police officer said calmly. "A car matching Hazeleigh's was seen leaving the fort this morning. We just want to talk to Hazeleigh. That's all. I don't want to cause a scene, Zara, but I will if I have to."

"She isn't home. I already told you. And you came up here sirens blazing, so don't give me that BS about you just wanting to talk."

"Sure looks like her car sitting there, matching the description we were given," the cop said, ignoring her complaint about his sirens.

"Let's just go on over and see then," Landon suggested, pointing the two deputies toward Hazeleigh's cabin. "No harm in knocking on the door, is there?" he said to Zara, trying to remain cool under the circumstances.

He was practiced at pretend genial Southern charm.

He started leading the cops over to the cabin despite Zara's spluttering objections. He wished he could assure Zara he knew where Hazeleigh was and that this was some very strange misunderstanding, but for now he had to put himself between Zara and the officers and let them knock on Hazeleigh's door. As he did, Brody pulled up in his truck, and Jake and Cal appeared over the rise on their horses.

Making it clear Kate had been calling in reinforcements.

Brody came over to stand with Landon and Zara, while Cal and Jake disappeared into the stables, but they would no doubt be up here once they secured their horses.

When there was no answer from inside the cabin, one of the deputies turned to Zara.

"Why don't you let us in, Zara?"

"Why don't you—"

"You'd need a search warrant for that, wouldn't you?" Landon interrupted, trying to keep his voice casual—friendly, even. "Just to make sure it's all on the up-and-up?"

The cop was very quiet for a moment. "I hope you all know this doesn't look good for her."

"It doesn't look good for you harassing innocent people," Zara returned.

"If any of you see Hazeleigh, I'm going to need a phone call. She has to come in. Just for some questions."

"Does Thomas know about you dropping by?" Zara demanded, mentioning her cousin, who was also a Bent County deputy.

"Thomas isn't my boss, Zara."

"Neither is your mom, but I don't see that stopping you from—"

Jake easily stepped in between Zara and the deputy, but he didn't address the lawman—he spoke to Zara. "Come on now," he said quietly. "We don't need to make this a scene."

"Maybe I want to," Zara said, glaring at the cop over Jake's shoulder.

"I know you do, but let's think about Hazeleigh," Jake said quietly. "We've got to find her."

Landon kept his mouth shut, but he was very much on Zara's side for this one.

With Jake's interference taking Zara's attention off him, the cop stepped away.

"I'm calling Thomas," Zara said. "I'm going to get to the bottom of this." She looked at the cabin and where

Landon was still standing near the door. "Where could she be? What if she's in danger, too?"

Landon felt badly for keeping his mouth shut, but Hazeleigh had been right. Those cops might just want to ask questions at the moment, but if someone had called in that Hazeleigh's car had been leaving the scene…things would get complicated. Delicate.

It was best if he was the only one who knew where Hazeleigh was until they got to the bottom of what was going on.

Chapter Three

Being alone in the old, dilapidated schoolhouse did not do much for Hazeleigh's peace of mind. It simply gave time for panic to multiply. Minutes felt like hours. Hours felt like minutes.

She was no good at subterfuge. At lying. She did not charge through with a plan—that was Zara's department. Hazeleigh knew herself *very* well, and none of her talents were ones that would allow her to handle this with aplomb.

It was why escape and running away was the only answer. It was why, back when she'd been held for Amberleigh's murder, she'd preferred jail over telling Zara everything she knew.

At her core, Hazeleigh knew she was a coward. Her two older sisters—even if only by minutes—had gotten all the bravery and verve, the strength and hardheadedness.

Before Mom had died, she'd always said Hazeleigh was as soft as dandelion fluff. It had been a good thing when Mom said it. But it hadn't felt good since, and that had been over fifteen years ago now.

"This is such a mess," she muttered aloud, because

it felt good to fill the air with something other than dust motes.

Although... She frowned as she looked around. The floors were oddly...not clean, exactly, but free of the debris that should have built up over the years. That window should have been grimier—especially with the crack in it.

Maybe someone had been taking care of it? Maybe even Mr. Field. Or maybe there was a Peterson hiding about?

If someone had been here, though, and recently, she wasn't safe. They could come back at any moment, assuming it wasn't Mr. Field. But someone could come. They'd call the police, and she wouldn't have time to run.

She had to get out. Now. She could not wait for Landon, promises or not. She grabbed her backpack, but before she could get both arms through the straps the door was creaking open.

She nearly screamed, searching the area for a weapon to ward off whoever was coming to find her. But she found nothing that could cause blunt-force trauma—something she probably wouldn't have been able to go through with, anyway.

But it was Landon, of course, easily and almost soundlessly sliding inside the building. Nothing to scream about.

But his face told her everything she needed to know about what had gone on with the cops.

"They came to arrest me."

"Question you," he corrected.

But she knew too well where questions led. Especially questions with no good answers. And she had *no* good answers.

"I want you to tell me everything that happened. Starting with when you got the message from Mr. Field."

While his authoritative voice was something of a comfort—it was nice *someone* thought they knew what to do—she knew he was wrong. She shook her head. "It doesn't matter. I have been *through* this. I know how it goes. I can't answer the questions the way they want me to, and I am dead meat."

"Hazeleigh, someone made a call to the police."

"What do you mean?"

"The deputy said someone called about seeing your car leave the fort." He frowned at the cracked chalkboard. "But that'd be normal, wouldn't it? You leave in your car? Why would someone call the cops about that?"

"I don't know. I don't keep normal hours. It wouldn't be of note, unless the police were asking around."

But Landon shook his head. "The cop said someone *called*. That doesn't sound right. It doesn't add up."

"You think…someone is trying to make it look like I did it?"

"Wouldn't be the first time, would it?"

"I was complicit in being framed last time. I let the police arrest me because I knew I'd be safer." She clasped her hands together to keep herself from screaming or running or both. "I can't do it again. It won't work like last time, and Jake ended up shot anyway. I have to leave."

"Let's take it one step at a time. Right now, they want to question you because of a phone call."

"I won't. I can't."

Landon nodded, and she knew he was purposefully keeping space between them. Purposefully holding up his hands. She understood the Thompson brothers had all very consciously decided to give her a wide berth.

Because she was *skittish*.

That old feeling of jealousy welled up inside her. That she couldn't be more like brazen Amberleigh or certain Zara.

But Amberleigh was dead, wasn't she? That's what being brazen had gotten her. Zara had turned out all right, she supposed, but Hazeleigh knew that wishing she was more like her sister was pointless. They were just different…and she loved Zara. She wanted her to be happy after all she'd done to try to protect Hazeleigh over the years.

"I want to know more before we do anything," Landon said. And Hazeleigh didn't miss the *we*, which made no sense to her. "About this call. About the murder. But I don't think you should run away. Keep a low profile here, sure, but you could be in danger."

"Why would…" She swallowed at the lump in her throat. It was silly to ask him why he'd help her.

She had spent her childhood dreaming of knights in shining armor. Men who swooped in to help, like a cowboy in the old west. She loved a noble, good-hearted hero.

She'd stopped believing in them at some point, put away fictional ideas of good men, but then the Thompson brothers had shown up last year. Jake had stepped in to help Zara, before he'd meant anything to her. They'd all rallied around Kate to help her. The Thompson brothers were just the kind of men who felt they should help.

Hazeleigh was still having a hard time going back to believing in good guys, but still she knew Landon was one of them.

"Why would I help?" Landon smiled at her. It was a kind smile. A handsome smile. Still, he kept his distance. "Your sister is marrying my brother. That makes us family, more or less. She is going to say yes, isn't she?"

Hazeleigh knew he was trying to draw her into a conversation about something else. Distract her from all the problems at hand. Still, he was so kind about it, she could only let him. "She better."

Landon chuckled. "Yeah? Why do you say that?"

"I love Zara with everything I am. I'd be lost without her. But she is *not* an easy woman. I can't imagine anyone but Jake putting up with her."

Landon grinned. "Jake's had lots of experience with difficult. He's dealt with Cal all these years without punching him."

Hazeleigh smiled in return. "Cal is definitely…" She struggled to come up with the words for Landon's taciturn brother.

"A SOB?"

She laughed. She couldn't help it, even though it was mean. And not altogether true. She thought of Cal as more…troubled than mean. A control freak, but she'd watched Zara try to control things in a similar fashion.

That sort of behavior was often born out of…well, desperation more than anything else.

But his brothers and her sister aside, there was really only one solution to her problem.

"I appreciate you trying to distract me, Landon, and wanting to help, but the best thing for me to do is run. Really. I've had time to think, to calm myself. It might not be safe to stay here. This is all a part of Mr. Field's research, and I just… I don't know why anyone would kill him, but when the police look into what he's working on, someone might come looking here."

"You can't run, Hazeleigh," Landon said, gently enough, but she didn't particularly like him telling her what to do. "They'll only follow." He looked around the schoolhouse. "We'll figure this out. Together."

We. Together.

Hazeleigh didn't have the faintest idea what to say to that.

HAZELEIGH GAPED AT him in a weighted silence that Landon let go on for as long as he could, which wasn't long. "I can hardly leave you to fend for yourself. Running is no joke, Hazeleigh, trust me. What's more, I know you don't want to do that to Zara."

Her frown deepened. "You don't understand."

She had no idea how much he understood. Maybe he hadn't had to run in the traditional sense, but this wasn't his life. He was living a fake life because a terrorist organization would want him dead otherwise.

Maybe he was making the best of this life, but he was still…a runaway. A hideaway.

"Give me a few days, okay? Just to get to the bottom

of what the police think; who made that call. Give me a few days." He kept his steady gaze on hers. Calm. But he wasn't feeling much of that underneath the veneer. He felt a little desperate. A lot angry.

Here was a sweet woman, who helped an old man do silly research, mostly kept to herself and never hurt anyone, he'd be willing to wager. And she kept getting dragged into other people's drama, likely because she was sweet and kept herself a bit apart.

"I'll stay close," he continued when she said nothing. He kept his shoulders loose and his mouth curved in an encouraging smile. But he couldn't quite get the message to his hand to unclench from its fist.

"You can't stay out here with me. People would notice you missing. I don't want anyone else to know, to lie for me. I don't… I should do this on my own."

He wanted to scowl. It felt an ugly kind of familiar. All the ways he'd tried to help every single member of his family to get out from his father's thumb, or escape all the trouble they'd gotten themselves into.

Not one person had accepted his help. And look where they'd all ended up? "You're innocent. You should have help. I'm not going to tell anyone else. Not yet. I won't be here with you 24/7, no, but I'm going to keep tabs and make sure you're safe and hidden here. Any poking around I do people will chalk up to you being Zara's sister, or me being a little sweet on you."

"Sweet on me," she echoed, her cheeks turning a pretty shade of pink.

He shouldn't have said that. Now was not the time for the truth, no matter how it was wrapped up in a joke. He shrugged easily, keeping his tone light. "Sure.

You're pretty. I'm a man. That's what some people will assume. No harm in it."

"But…I have terrible taste in men," she blurted.

Since he knew one of those men, he could hardly argue with her. That doctor she'd dated hadn't just been an absolute jerk, he'd been a murderer. And since he felt bad about her thinking about *that*, he grinned. "Maybe I don't have terrible taste in women."

Her mouth dropped open a little, and a little sound came out, but otherwise she said nothing, which was probably for the best. For both of them.

"Let's focus on the task at hand. Tell me exactly what happened."

Chapter Four

Hazeleigh was so rattled by this whole conversation that she went ahead and told him everything. From waking up to Mr. Field's message, to finding him dead.

A little sweet on you. She kept hearing him say it, in that faint Southern drawl, and she didn't know what to do with it.

Surely, he was joking. Trying to lighten the mood. If he was *sweet* on her...

Well, he wasn't. So she needed to focus.

"Was anyone ever overly interested in Mr. Field's research?" Landon asked. He still kept his distance, but he wasn't still. He walked around the schoolhouse, studying the window, the screw holes where desks used to be drilled into the floors, the cracks in the plaster walls.

"What would constitute 'overly interested'?"

"Lots of questions from someone. Strange attention to something seemingly minor. Meetups. Et cetera."

Hazeleigh shook her head. "I don't think you understand how history buffs work. Mr. Field was always exchanging emails—asking questions, answering questions. He wrote and argued on message boards. He was involved in a few Facebook groups—though I had to do most of that for him as he claimed it was too complicated for him to learn."

Landon nodded, though his expression reflected puzzlement. "Okay. We'll have to make a list." He continued to move about the room, talking about next steps and prioritizing, and all Hazeleigh could do was watch.

He was taking over, and there was a part of her—that forever-a-coward part—that wanted to relax into it. Thank God someone else wanted to take over.

But part of her knew it was wrong. She had to handle this herself. No matter how nice or noble Landon might be, he shouldn't get mixed up in her running away.

"Landon, I don't want you…"

He turned to face her and she…lost all the words. The denials. Because she very much wanted him to… Well, she didn't know quite yet. Just that she wanted him here because the thought of being alone right now terrified her.

He waited for her to finish her sentence. And waited. She struggled to find the words, especially when he was watching her intently, as if her answer was important. Like the wrong one might disappoint him.

"I should do this alone," she said, trying to be firm and as certain as he was. "You don't want to entangle yourself in it."

Landon shrugged. "Too late. Now, let's talk about this phone call."

"Landon."

"We can bicker about it later when time isn't of the essence. Now, does anyone live close enough to the fort to have seen you go to or leave the parking lot?"

"No."

"Not even if they had binoculars or a telescope or something?"

She shook her head. "Nothing. Someone would have had to have been on the road. Or in the fort itself." Someone had called the police about seeing her car. She still couldn't process that information. The fort was isolated. It was rare to get visitors without a big advertised event—and even when they did get the random visitor, it wouldn't have been so early in the morning, a good two hours before the fort opened to the public.

She'd gone in and found Mr. Field dead, and someone had seen her. Seen her leave. Upset and in a hurry. That *would* look bad.

But why would someone be looking? Who had alerted the police that Mr. Field was dead in the first place?

"We need to know who alerted the police," Landon said. "It doesn't add up that someone found him *and* saw you leave."

"You think…it could be whoever killed Mr. Field?"

"We just don't know until we know who called and where they called from. I'll need my computer."

She knew Landon was some kind of computer whiz. He'd helped Kate get to the bottom of her family troubles, but… "Landon—"

He held up a hand. "No more arguments, Hazeleigh. This is where we are. We can either work together, which will yield much faster results, or I can tell Zara where you are."

She frowned. It was like some kind of ultimatum, when she had repeatedly told him she didn't want his help. "That isn't a fair either-or."

He smiled gently. "I never said I was fair."

"You can't just—"

He pulled his cell phone out of his back pocket. "Okay. Zara it is."

She practically leaped forward in an attempt to grab the phone out of his hand. Of course, he held firm, and she ended up in a pointless tug-of-war she wasn't going to win.

She huffed out a breath and glared at him.

His mouth quirked. Clearly he was not intimidated by her. Clearly she *amused* him. She wanted to be mad about it, but it was hard to blame him. She was the opposite of intimidating.

But she could do other things…even if she couldn't physically intimidate.

"It isn't right to bring Zara into this. You know that. She'll worry. She'll fume. She'll probably get *herself* tossed in jail trying to prove I didn't do it."

Landon's mouth firmed and Hazeleigh knew she'd scored a point.

"In fact, if she was with the police, I'm willing to bet she was yelling at them and someone—likely Jake— had to step in and stop her from doing something rash."

He said nothing. Hazeleigh nodded her head as if he'd confirmed her suspicions. "I know my sister. She can't handle this with an even temper or a cool head. I think you understand—I *hope* you understand—that it's a situation that needs both. I panicked a little bit in the beginning."

"You found your boss, your *friend*, murdered. Of course you did."

She didn't *need* him to make her feel better about

that, but it did ease some stress inside of her. That she hadn't reacted completely wrongly. Or maybe it just made her sad all over again so she didn't feel the stress.

"If you promise to sit tight," Landon said, "I'll see what I can do about finding some answers, okay?"

"I can't promise… You need to understand. I don't regret running, even if it *was* panic. I knew I'd be blamed for it, whether that's my weird intuition or just having the sense God gave me, I don't know. But I *knew* I'd be blamed. And I refuse to sit around in a cell while everyone else tries to save me again."

Landon shook his head. "That doesn't mean running is the answer, Hazeleigh."

"What other answer is there?"

"Fighting for the truth. Why can't we all help you fight for the truth?"

"We have to keep everyone out of this. If I can't keep you out, that's… Well, it's already happened. But I can't drag Zara into it. I can't."

"She'd support you."

"She'd *fight* for me, Landon. And I know I'm lucky to have a sister who would, but I don't need a fight. I just need…to disappear."

"No, Hazeleigh, you need the truth. I'm damn good at finding it. Stay put. Let me get to the bottom of this for you."

"How is that different than jail, Landon? Hiding here while you do all the work?"

"Because you're going to help me do the work. You're going to do some of that fighting yourself."

That sounded…better than the other options she'd thought of, but… "How?"

"Just stay put, and I'll show you." Then he was gone.

Leaving her alone. And conflicted.

LANDON'S BIGGEST CHALLENGE was going to be explaining his absences. He could look into Mr. Field's murder easily enough. Like he'd told Hazeleigh, everyone would think he was helping out because their families had connections. His brothers would likely give him that look that told him they knew—even if Hazeleigh didn't—that he paid a little too close attention there.

Neither reason bothered him.

He stabled his horse. He'd disappeared again after the cops had left by giving the excuse he'd ride the property and see if he could find any trace of Hazeleigh. He knew he'd have to lie to Zara, and he had no trouble lying to people. But when he knew someone was worried, and he could ease that worry with the truth, that made the lying harder.

Before he even was up the porch steps, Zara had the door open. She stood there at the threshold of the old ranch house. "Any sign of her?" she demanded.

Since he'd already been preparing himself, he managed an apologetic smile. "Sorry." Zara frowned, but she held open the door for him and he stepped into the living room. Almost everyone was situated around the room. Cal stood in the threshold between kitchen and living room. Kate and Brody sat next to each other on a couch, Jake on an armchair. Zara paced. The only two people missing were Henry and Dunne.

"Did you guys find anything here?" Landon asked, hoping to take the focus off himself.

"Zara went through the cabin," Jake offered. "Hazeleigh had taken some things. Not just her everyday work things, but personal belongings and cash savings. It's likely she was spooked, but she wasn't taken or harmed," Jake said, watching Zara the whole time.

"I don't know where she could have gone—would have gone." Zara wrung her hands as she paced. Landon could tell she was trying to keep a strong facade, but worry had dug lines into her forehead, and her eyes were sad. The angry warrior of earlier had softened into a sister worried for her sister's safety. "There's no family or friends to go to. Unless she went to Thomas, and he's not telling me."

"We could always make an impromptu stop by his place in Bent," Brody suggested. "Maybe she's with him and didn't want..." He trailed off, pulling a slight face.

Kate rolled her eyes. "You stopped about three words too late," she muttered.

"Didn't want *what*?" Zara demanded.

Brody raised an eyebrow, causing Zara to scowl.

"Let's try to be methodical about this," Cal said. As the former commander of Team Breaker, he was used to taking charge. No amount of time being here, being equals and out of the military, could get him out of the habit of trying to take control of a situation.

"Hazeleigh is *missing*," Zara retorted. "I don't need methodical. I don't need patience. I need to know my sister is safe."

It was a difficult thing for Landon not to say anything or give anything away. He wanted to offer Zara *some* reassurance, but he couldn't. Not yet. He'd find a way.

"I'm going to do some digging into what the cops know but aren't telling us," Landon said. Maybe he sounded a bit like Cal, trying to take over, but so be it. "If you could get any information out of your cousin that would be great, but the bottom line is someone called the cops saying they saw Hazeleigh leaving the fort. Why would anyone call about that? It's not out of the ordinary, and they'd have to have known there was something bad inside to call the police. It doesn't add up."

"Someone's framing her?" Kate asked.

"We don't know until we figure out who called. That's step one." Landon held up a hand before Zara could start in. "I know you want to find her, and you want to make sure she's safe. I get that. But she took things from her cabin, right? And she's been in this position before. She knows they could take her in, right? Why wouldn't she run away to avoid that?"

"Without telling me?" Zara demanded.

"Maybe she's protecting you," Jake said softly. Zara whirled on him, but she didn't say anything when he got up and put his hands on her shoulders. "Just like you'd protect her."

Zara huffed out a breath and leaned into Jake. "You all know Hazeleigh. She's too sweet, too soft and a damn sight too skittish to be off running away when there's no one for her to run to."

Landon didn't have a clue why that estimation of

Hazeleigh bothered him. It wasn't far off the mark, but he couldn't keep his mouth shut all the same. "Maybe you need to give her some credit, Zara."

"I'm not *not* giving her credit," Zara replied, but not with her usual anger. There was a softness to the denial, like she was afraid that's exactly what she was doing.

"I think it's clear she was scared, and why wouldn't she be? She's been through this before. So we do what we can to give her a reason not to be scared."

"I'm not going to quit looking for her."

Landon nodded, wondering how he'd keep Zara from searching the ranch. "No, we don't have to do that. But we should be careful we aren't leading the cops to her."

"She didn't do it," Kate said firmly from her seat on the couch. "Even if she was capable of murder, she never would have shot a gun. She hates guns. And she loves…" Kate swallowed, tears filling her eyes, though they didn't fall. "Mr. Field," she finally said.

Kate worked at the fort, so she also worked closely with Mr. Field.

"When was the last time you heard from Mr. Field?" Landon asked. What he really wanted to ask was if she'd also received a middle-of-the-night message from Mr. Field, but he couldn't ask without outing himself.

"Yesterday at work. He was closeted in his office, so I didn't pop in to say goodbye because he was deep in research mode." Brody slid his arm around Kate and she leaned into him. "It doesn't make any sense. He was an old man. Why would someone murder him like that?"

"We're going to figure it out," Landon assured her.

He looked at Cal, who was staring at him with some suspicion. But Landon wouldn't let that get to him.

He was going to get to the bottom of it all, one way or another.

Chapter Five

Hazeleigh spent the next few hours talking herself in and out of leaving. The thing that kept her in the old schoolhouse was the fact she couldn't think of a reliable way of getting away. They'd be looking for her car if she took it—and any of the Thompsons' vehicles if she got the guts to steal one of their ranch trucks. A horse wouldn't take her far enough, and she wouldn't be able to feed it long enough or be assured the horse would be cared for if she needed to leave it behind.

Cabs and ride shares were few and far between out here in the middle of nowhere, so she'd be noticed. Someone could call the cops.

Staying and accepting Landon's help seemed to be her only sensible option.

At least for now. Running was always a possibility if things went badly. Even if she had to do it on foot.

She spent some time sitting down and breathing, meditating over the situation before her. She let herself imagine what it might be like to go to the police. Express her innocence and hope for the best.

But thinking it—imagining it—left her with the same blind panic she'd first felt. Deep in her bones, whatever it was that told her bad things were coming was warning against letting the law handle it.

She thought about what Landon had said. That she'd be doing some of the fighting herself.

She'd never fought a day in her life. She hated confrontation. Avoided it. Ignored it. Ran away from it.

Wasn't right now an excellent example?

But Landon had made it sound so possible. He'd *show* her. The idea left her feeling…strange. It was a new feeling, amid all this old hat fear and running. Unsettled, but not the kind that made her want to retreat. This was something more she wanted to lean into.

It wasn't that she *liked* being a coward, it was just…it had often been the best way to handle her father growing up. Or even the best way to handle poor Amberleigh's temper. And the few times she'd been brave enough to stand up for herself, Zara had swooped in and taken the brunt of the reaction. Hazeleigh had never learned how to be the one who fought.

You're going to do some of that fighting yourself. Maybe she didn't know how, but Landon *had* said he'd show her how. The idea of that did not give her a bad feeling, did not send her into a panic.

But how did someone fight a lie? Or public opinion? Or whatever it was against her? She sat in the now dark schoolhouse and mulled things over.

Information. Facts. She was good at all those things. Organizing. Analyzing. Drawing conclusions. She just needed…

The door squeaked, moved. She had only a second of fear before she heard Landon's voice whispering assurances as a dark shadow slid into the room.

And then light.

The small camping lantern didn't offer enough light to see the whole room, but enough to make out Landon. He had a laptop under his arm, and a small backpack.

"You're probably starving," he offered, setting the pack between them.

She hadn't thought about food. Or sleep. She'd been too tied in knots to feel anything but the stress of the day.

"I had to be careful about what I took so no one notices and asks why I'm taking more food than usual." He pulled out a plastic snack bag full of nuts. An apple. A water bottle and a can of Zara's favorite pop.

Something about the whole thing made her want to cry. Because even though Landon was insisting on helping her, until this very moment she'd still felt very much alone. Separated.

But Landon hadn't just brought his laptop and the idea they were going to get to the bottom of Mr. Field's murder, he'd brought her food.

"Go on now and eat something," he insisted, pushing the supplies at her. "And I'll catch you up to speed."

Hazeleigh followed his instructions. Another one of her strengths. As she munched on the apple and sipped some water, she *did* begin to feel less shaky and untethered—even if she still didn't feel hungry through the knots in her stomach.

"Poked around a bit in the police database, and Zara talked to Thomas and he told her a few basic things, but nothing much. Still, that phone call was an anonymous tip that something bad had happened at the fort, and your car had been seen driving away. The cops are looking into it, as they aren't totally sold on an anonymous tip when it comes to murder. I know you've already made up your mind, but right now the police view you as a person of interest, not a suspect."

He was looking at her carefully in the dim light of the lantern. He wanted her to turn herself in. The apple turned to a lump in her throat, and she had a difficult time swallowing it down. When she spoke, her voice was shaky at best. "I can't turn myself in now." There was no sensible way to explain it to him. "I just…can't."

Landon nodded, and she was surprised that he didn't argue with her. He pointed to the nuts. "Eat those, too," he said instead, before continuing his explanation of what he'd found out.

"There weren't signs of a struggle according to the report I managed to get my eyes on. But the office was a mess. So not necessarily a defending-himself struggle. But a mess. Did Mr. Field keep anything valuable in his office someone might have been after?"

Hazeleigh sipped her water and sighed. "Unfortunately the only answer I have is maybe. He was a disorganized soul—that's why he paid me to keep track of things, organize them. His office was often full of random things. Sometimes he'd stuff cash in his desk. Sometimes he'd leave it in his car. But nothing specific. Nothing… I'd think if someone really wanted money, they would have gone to his house. He didn't trust banks."

"Is there anything other than cash someone might want their hands on?"

Hazeleigh tried to think. Mr. Field collected historical artifacts—some were rare and valuable. Occasionally people contacted him wanting to buy them from him, but Mr. Field never sold. He couldn't part with anything—from scraps of paper to sentimental matchsticks. "It's possible? But it also seems far-fetched."

Landon nodded thoughtfully, then pointed at the bag of nuts again. "All of it," he instructed.

Hazeleigh wasn't the biggest fan of pistachios, but she knew this wasn't about what she liked to eat. It was about keeping her strength up. If he had to be careful about the food he brought, she had to be smart and eat whatever he brought.

"So the police think someone was after something?"

"I don't know what the police think. That's my interpretation. Based on what little information was in the report, and what even less information Thomas gave Zara. A mess that wasn't about a self-defense fight has to be someone looking for *something*."

Hazeleigh's stomach sank. "That just makes me an even bigger suspect. I'm the one person in the world who knows what he has."

"But wouldn't you know *where*?"

"It just depends, but I'm willing to bet those are the exact questions the police would ask me. Do I keep track? Does he hide things? Are any valuable? And it would all come back on me. No matter what."

Landon's mouth firmed, but he didn't argue with her. "That's why we need to know if anything was taken. Or even what the focus of the search was. If we know what, we can prove that you wouldn't want or need whatever it is."

Hazeleigh wasn't convinced that would prove her

innocence, but it seemed like a step in the right direction. "How are we going to do that?"

"Well, we're going to break into a crime scene. If you're up to it."

HAZELEIGH SPLUTTERED ON the sip of water she'd just taken. Landon winced. Perhaps he should have timed that statement a little better. "I'd say you don't have to go with me, but I need your eyes."

Once she was done coughing, she shook her head. "I don't understand."

"If we can get into Mr. Field's office, which presumably you had a hand in organizing, you could see what is missing, or messed with. You're the only one who might be able to figure out what the murderer was after."

Hazeleigh chewed on her bottom lip for a moment, and Landon had to busy himself with zipping up the backpack rather than allowing himself to be distracted by her mouth.

"What if I can't? What if it's just a mess and I don't know anything?"

Landon shrugged, risking a look back at her. She wasn't chewing on her lip anymore, but her eyebrows were furrowed and her dark eyes were lost.

It made his heart twist in his chest. "Look, to get to the bottom of something you sometimes take a few steps that don't get you anywhere. That's okay."

"What if we get caught?"

He offered her his most reassuring smile. "We won't."

"You can't guarantee that," she said with an expression that reminded him of a scolding schoolteacher.

Why he found *that* attractive was beyond him, and he couldn't quite keep the charm out of his drawl.

"Trust me."

She didn't smile back, or even blush and look away like she might have a few weeks ago. She held his gaze, her eyes heartbreakingly serious.

"I do trust you."

Her answer hit him too hard, but he was also good at hiding his emotions when something hit far too hard. "Good," he replied.

She sighed, looking down at the last handful of nuts. "I don't want these."

He held out his hand and she transferred them into his palm, their fingers brushing briefly. If she felt any of that buzz of electricity he did, she hid it well.

Which shouldn't irritate him as much as it did. He tossed the nuts into his mouth and crunched hard enough to keep his mind on the important task at hand. "They'll have the office taped off, but I'm willing to bet they don't have someone stationed out there overnight. We'll head over now."

"How?"

"I've got the horses waiting. I've never seen you ride, but Zara always says you're capable."

"Yes, I can ride," she said, a thread of insult running through her tone. "I *did* grow up on a ranch."

"You're not exactly dressed for it."

She looked down at her skirt and frothy, vintage sweater in the dim light. Then she looked up at him, angling her chin slightly so that she reminded him of Zara—a rare feat, no matter how much the sisters looked alike. "A true rider doesn't need *pants*, Landon."

There was really something wrong with him that the primness in her tone affected him the way it did.

He could not focus on that right now. "So we'll ride over. I'll scope out the area, and then we'll see what we can do to get inside. If we've got the opportunity, we'll do it tonight. If not, we'll make a plan to go back."

"How long do you honestly think I can hide out here?"

He didn't touch her as a rule, but this seemed like the kind of thing that needed a connection. Even if it was just his hands on her shoulders.

Of course, that reminded him that Jake had done the same to Zara, and they were in a committed romantic relationship. He was just a friend, at best, offering a helping hand.

They started that way.

He pushed away the thought, gave her shoulder one squeeze then let go. "As long as it takes," he said firmly. A promise. Maybe something closer to a vow.

Her expression was pained. Worried. "Do you really think—"

Frustrated he couldn't seem to get through to her, he cut her off. "Hazeleigh, I wouldn't be doing any of it if I didn't think it was worth a shot. Look, I know how to…" He wasn't sure what the right words were. There was an entire decade of experience he couldn't tell her about. "It's not going out on a limb. I know how to assess a situation, and I'm not about to put you in the middle of anything dangerous or that might get you caught before we have enough information to make sure you're not the suspect."

"I'm not worried about…danger," she said, clearly picking that word very carefully.

"Then what are you worried about?"

She shook her head. "I don't…know. It just doesn't feel right. None of it feels right. Except…" This time when she trailed off, he didn't think it was because she didn't have the words, but because she was stopping herself from saying them.

"Except what?"

She wasn't looking at him anymore. She had her gaze down on her fingers, all twisted together in anxiety. "I trust you, Landon," was all she said. Quietly. Almost…shyly, as if trusting him was some great admission, even though she'd mentioned it once before.

But, he supposed, if he put it all together, she was saying the only thing that felt right was that she trusted him. And that meant far more than it should.

"You don't think your brothers will notice you missing?" she asked.

"If they do, I'll just tell them the truth. Without you in it. I went to the fort. *I* looked around."

"So we're going to ride our horses over to the fort in the middle of the night. We're going to break into a crime scene. I'm going to somehow figure out what the murderer might have been after. Then we're going to prove to the police that I'm innocent by…"

Tracking down the murderer, Landon thought to himself. But he wasn't about to say that out loud. Not yet. Besides, she wouldn't necessarily be involved in that part. If he could help it.

"Let's take everything one step at a time. The first step is to ride over to the fort and see what's what. You're a local girl. Surely you know a shortcut."

She bristled again, like when he'd mentioned her outfit for riding. "Of course I know a shortcut."

He didn't smile, though he wanted to. He liked those little flashes of pride and temper. She should let them out more often.

"So that's the first step. Ready?"

Some of the worry crept in around the pride, but Landon watched carefully as she steeled herself. She clenched her fingers and let them go, straightened her shoulders, then gave a firm nod.

Because underneath all that…skittishness she wore like a shield, she was a fighter. She just didn't give herself enough credit for that yet.

Maybe at the end of this, when they'd proven she was innocent, she would.

Chapter Six

Hazeleigh could admit here, in the middle of the night, on the back of her horse, that she'd missed riding Buttercup. She'd missed feeling like the ranch was part of her. She didn't want to be a rancher, never had, but she'd grown up in the pastures and fields. She'd loved and lost horses and dogs and cats. She liked ranch *life*, even if she wasn't cut out for the work.

When the Thompson brothers bought the ranch last year, she'd felt like she couldn't enjoy the ranch anymore. Even the cabin that she'd shared with Zara before Zara moved into the main house with Jake was just a rental.

She should be over it, let it go, but it still irked. Dad had sold it all out from under them without even a second thought or apology. He'd considered it his right. His *due*. His wife had died, and he'd had to raise his triplet daughters alone, only to have his favorite kid run away at sixteen. Why shouldn't he take a bigger payoff than the ranch deserved and leave?

Hazeleigh inhaled sharply. It wasn't any good getting angry with her father all over again. What was done was done. She couldn't change it and being angry didn't help. It only made her feel…well, angry. And anger was never a thing she knew what to do with. It sat there in her stomach, churning like acid.

The night whirred and chirped with nocturnal life. The stars above shone like a quilt of glitter, so big and vast. All those things settled in her bones like they always did. Contentment. Hope. Belonging.

She'd never understood why Amberleigh had such a driving need to leave when they were young. This was home. Built on generations of hard work and tragedy and all that hope.

No, Hazeleigh didn't really want to run away from her problems. Not when Wilde and the ranch were home, ownership or not. It simply felt like it might be the only option. The best option for both her and Zara.

But if Landon really could prove she wasn't the murderer…

She breathed out a sigh. That was a big *if.* "The highway is coming up," she said softly to Landon. "We'll have to cross it to get to the fort."

"All right. Let's get off the horses and lead them."

They both dismounted and Landon came to stand next to Hazeleigh, horses bracketing them in the moonlight. They walked the next few yards, leading their horses by the reins.

When they reached the ditch before the highway, Landon paused. "I'll cross first," he said. "Then I'll give a whistle when it's your turn."

"You don't think we should cross together?"

"I know it's a pretty low-trafficked highway, but we can't be too careful. Someone comes by and sees me cross, you'll have time to get away."

"And leave you here?" What kind of coward did he take her for? She was at least a *loyal* coward.

"I'm not a person of interest in a murder case, far as I know, so I should make out okay even if I get caught."

Hazeleigh didn't correct him out loud. Just in her head. She wasn't a *person of interest*, no matter what the cops said. She was a *suspect*.

Still, she didn't think she could just…ditch Landon, even if he could talk his way out of trouble. He probably could. Flash a grin, really amp up the Southern drawl and anyone would fall under his spell. But she wouldn't want to leave him to deal with it. She couldn't.

Hopefully it wouldn't come to that.

The highway was dark, quiet. Hazeleigh didn't expect to see anyone except maybe a random semitruck, but even that was unlikely as this was a two-lane road that ran parallel to the bigger interstate closer to town.

Landon crossed first. She listened as his horse's hooves clip-clopped against the hard surface of the road. She petted Buttercup as she waited for Landon's whistle. When it sounded, she took a deep breath. She looked up and down the highway and saw no sign of any lights or vehicles.

She crossed, *knowing* no one was going to pop up, and yet she held her breath, her heart pounding in her chest louder than Buttercup's horseshoes hitting the pavement.

She made it to the other side. No one appeared. Nothing happened.

"How much farther you think?" Landon asked.

"Not much. Maybe a quarter of a mile. We'll come up on the back of the cabin side of the fort."

"All right. Lead the way."

He held Buttercup's reins as she mounted her horse, then got up on his in an easy, fluid moment.

"You're good with horses."

He smiled, his large, scarred hand moving across his horse's flank in all that silvery moonlight. "Yeah, we get along all right." He urged his horse into a forward walk and Hazeleigh did the same.

"Zara said you guys didn't know much about ranching when you got here."

"I suppose we didn't. She was a great help."

No further explanation. Hazeleigh knew she could press, but she held herself back. There were more important things to accomplish tonight.

She urged Buttercup forward. Toward the fort. Toward… Her stomach churned, a mixture of anxiety and fear. An image of Mr. Field, slumped over his desk and bloody, flashed through her mind—unbidden—over and over again.

The fort and its buildings looked like they always did in the moonlight—stark and lonely against all the surrounding nothingness, with only the far-off shadow of mountains hinting at any Western roots.

"Let's tie the horses here, and then walk across the yard," Landon suggested. "Just to make sure the cops don't have anyone posted."

"Okay." Hazeleigh couldn't make out all the shapes in the dark, but it didn't look like there was anyone for miles around. They dismounted their horses and Landon tied both their reins to a post near the historic cabin.

There was a beat of hesitation and then Landon held

out his hand. "Just in case, we want to be absolutely silent. Hold my hand. Squeeze if you need anything."

She stood stock-still for a moment. She'd touched him or been touched by him more today than she'd been touched by *anyone* in the last few months. A purposeful choice on her part after everything with Douglas.

But this wasn't about her bad choices. This was about finding out the truth. She slid her hand into Landon's and felt a kind of…comfort or protection. Maybe her instincts were all wrong when it came to people, but Zara's weren't. And Zara trusted all of Jake's brothers, even uptight Cal, irritable Henry and taciturn Dunne.

Landon was the nicest out of all of them, except maybe Jake, and even then, it might be a tie. So… So this was fine. She could hold his hand and trust him to get her out of this mess.

She could always run away if it didn't go well. She had to keep that reminder in her back pocket. It was always important to have a Plan B.

They walked hand in hand across the yard between the cabin and main fort building. A surreal experience in the cold evening, pretty and magical even though danger seemed to lurk in every shadow.

"I don't see signs of anyone. We'll clear the tape and get in if we can, okay?" Landon whispered.

Hazeleigh could only nod as they inched closer and closer. She could see—and hear—the crime-scene tape now. It flapped in the breeze, a wiggling phantom in the light of the moon. Behind it was the fort.

Hazeleigh had loved this place. It was like a second home. An homage to a past that might have been tough and lonely and sad, but it couldn't change. It was what it was. Solid. Sturdy.

Now it was the place Mr. Field had been murdered. In his cluttered office, with his favorite possessions—documents and photographs from the past, some over a century old.

"I don't want to go in there." The words fell out. It wasn't a thought so much as a feeling—sudden and real and backed by panic. The panic didn't get a foothold though, because Landon kept her hand squeezed in his, and it felt like an anchor again.

"I know, but sometimes it's best to face the things we don't want to do. Especially if it helps us figure out what happened. Mr. Field seems like the kind of guy who'd want everyone to know what really happened."

He was. Absolutely. His entire life was studying an old bank-robbery story about gold that had mysteriously disappeared. He wanted answers.

And never found them.

"Just keep your hand in mine," Landon said reassuringly.

She did, and it made this whole horrible situation feel a little bit more survivable.

LANDON COULD FEEL the resistance in the way Hazeleigh held his hand. She was gripping it tight—something that surprised him even as they ducked under the crime-scene tape—but without much warning, she'd suddenly pull. Not against his hold, but against their forward progress.

He knew no one was here. Unfortunately, that didn't bode well for the police having another suspect aside from Hazeleigh. Hazeleigh wasn't the kind of suspect who went back to the scene of the crime. She was the kind of suspect who ran.

They reached the door of the fort.

"I have my key," Hazeleigh whispered beside him as he used his free hand to test the knob. He knew it would be locked, but he wanted to get a feel for what he was working with.

"I'd rather the cops think someone broke in if they figure out anyone was here at all. Using your key only keeps pointing the finger at you." Reluctantly, he dropped her hand. The knob was old. It bothered him the cops hadn't put up more security around the murder scene, but maybe they'd scrubbed it already. Gotten everything they needed.

He pulled his pocketknife out of his pocket and got to work on jimmying the lock. Once it clicked, he slowly pushed open the heavy door, trying to avoid any creaking sound.

"Should I ask where you learned to do that?" Hazeleigh asked, close at his back as he got the door open enough for them to slide in.

"A story for another time." They stepped inside the fort. The air was stale and smelled of commercial-grade cleaning products. The murder room had likely been scrubbed, but would they have taken everything in the office, making this entire trip a worthless enterprise?

Only one way to find out.

He pulled the small penlight out of his other cargo pocket and flashed it on. It offered a very narrow, dim line of light.

"Can you show me the way to his office?"

Hazeleigh audibly swallowed and didn't move.

"He's not in there. They likely cleaned everything up, too. That's what that smell is. Cleaner and bleach."

She nodded, but she still didn't move. He slid his arm around her shoulders. She seemed to be getting used to him taking his hand, letting him touch her shoulder. She didn't flinch or run away.

She trusted him. If he spent too much time thinking about that, he might be downright humbled.

But they didn't have time for that. He propelled her forward, getting her to take those first few steps, and then she led him toward the back. She paused at a door.

"Don't touch it," he instructed.

"If you're worried about fingerprints, mine are already here. Everywhere. Yours aren't."

"I can wipe mine. I did it out there."

"You did?"

He reached out and turned the knob. It wasn't locked either. This time, he slowed down his movements so she could see him wipe his prints.

She frowned as she watched, deep in thoughts she didn't verbalize. He pointed his light inside the office, making sure his body blocked her view until he was sure things were clean.

It was a tiny, windowless room. Though it was clear the office had been cleaned and things had been moved around, there were still a lot of things jammed into corners and drawers. He drew Hazeleigh inside.

Since there were no windows, he shut the door behind them and flipped on the light, making sure to wipe his prints again.

Hazeleigh stood with her back to the door, her face

as white as a sheet as she looked at the empty spot in front of the desk, where Mr. Field and the chair he was sitting on would have been this morning.

Landon weighed his options, and in the end he decided the quickest way to get through this was to push forward. It made his gut twist into knots, but the sooner they were finished, the sooner he could get her out of here.

"We have to keep in mind the police would have taken anything contaminated along with anything they thought was evidence."

"Contaminated," Hazeleigh echoed.

Landon worried she might throw up, her pallor turning a little green around the edges. But she breathed out as she took in the scene.

"Almost everything is here," Hazeleigh said, her voice thready. "Just the way it was. Except for what was on his desk, where…"

Landon nodded. That was strange. If Mr. Field had been shot in the office, if there had been as much blood as Hazeleigh had said, many more items should have been cleared out of this room.

"Any research that's a primary source, or historical document in any way, would have been kept in archival boxes or protectors. Since it's a historic site, the county likely would have sent someone over to make sure artifacts weren't cleaned or destroyed without inspection first."

She swallowed and then finally stepped forward, her gaze sweeping over the desk. "His computer is gone, obviously. He was slumped over it." She took a shuddering breath. "I don't know if he had anything on his desk in front of him. I didn't see. I didn't…"

Landon stepped forward and rested his hand on her shoulder. "It's okay. Whatever you saw or didn't. We're just getting an idea. If you don't remember, don't notice anything, that's all right."

She nodded. "I do all the organizing. Usually at the end of the day he leaves his desk a mess, and I come in and clean and file. Going by how I left things the night before, there's an entire box missing from right here," she said, pointing to a corner on the desk. "It held any photographs of the bank. Mr. Field's area of interest was the supposed bank robbery here back in 1892. He kept any and all real and photocopied pictures of the bank—past and present—in this box. There was also another photo album with pictures of sites people thought the stolen gold was hidden."

"Were the albums here when you came in this morning?"

"I don't…know."

"Okay, that's okay." He squeezed her shoulder in reassurance. He'd be able to hack into the photos the police took of the scene once they uploaded them to their system. He wouldn't put her through looking at the crime scene the way it had been found—with a bloody Mr. Field—but if he knew what to look for, that was a step.

"If he had things on his desk, it would have been… file folders from the cabinet over there. There was blood all over the desk, so the police would have… It would be ruined."

"Was there blood anywhere else?"

"I don't…" She swallowed and closed her eyes. "It's a blur. I can't…"

"Okay, let's focus on the here and now. Can you look through the filing cabinets and maybe see if anything's missing?"

She took another tentative step. With shaking hands, she touched the filing cabinet next to the desk. "We keep any newspaper or magazine articles, printouts of anything we've found online in the top drawer. Biographies of all involved in the second. The third door is random things Mr. Field thought might be related."

"Go ahead. Take a look."

She wiped her hands on the front of her jeans and then nodded. She pulled open the first one carefully and frowned. "There's a lot missing here."

"Could you make a list?"

The task seemed to steady her. She found a piece of paper and a pen and began to mutter to herself as she wrote. Landon watched the clock as she went through each drawer, her list growing and growing.

"I don't think it would make sense for the police to have taken all these, and Mr. Field wouldn't have had them *all* out on his desk."

"Then that's where we'll start."

She nodded, holding the list to her chest. "I don't know what we'll find."

"I don't either. But we'll go through, see if you can come up with some connections, and…" Landon paused. Something…wasn't right. "Don't say a word," he ordered, and flipped off the light, plunging them into darkness.

Chapter Seven

Hazeleigh wanted to scream. She bit her lip instead and was surprised to find herself reaching out for Landon's hand. But she needed that connection. That tether to reality and the reminder she couldn't just…crumble to the floor and wail at her bad luck.

She didn't know why he'd turned off the light suddenly, but she knew it couldn't be good.

So she stood completely still, holding on to Landon for dear life. He didn't move. He was as still as a statue himself.

Then she heard it—a creak, followed by a very faint shuffle.

A footstep.

She gripped Landon's hand harder. Bit her tongue harder. Everything inside of her screamed to react in some way, but she couldn't.

After another few moments passed and she heard nothing because her heart echoed so loudly in her ears. Landon pulled her from where she'd been standing by the filing cabinet. Gently, he moved her to the little corner on the same wall as the door. He kept maneuvering her until her back was pressed against the wall.

She realized that if someone opened the door, she would be effectively hidden by it. Landon leaned in, his mouth just about brushing her ear.

She narrowly swallowed down a squeak.

"Don't move," Landon said, his whisper barely audible even as she felt his breath against her cheek.

But then he tried to let go of her hand, and she didn't know what he planned to do, but she just knew… She just knew it was wrong. She *felt* it, the way she did sometimes. Whether it was a true feeling or not, she didn't know, but even after so many different ways she'd been burned, she still couldn't let people go out there into something that was *wrong*. So she held on to his hand for dear life rather than let it go.

She spoke once she trusted herself to keep her voice as quiet as his. "You stay right here."

"Haze—"

She pulled him closer, so that they were effectively chest to…well, he was quite a bit taller than her so it was more like her chest to his midsection. He didn't say anything, but Hazeleigh felt as though he was… fighting with himself. Deciding whether to stay close to her and the door that would hide both of them, or to find his own hiding spot. Or maybe he'd planned to go out there and face whatever they'd heard.

She didn't like any option that wasn't him, right here, with her. So she kept his hand in hers and used her free arm to curl around him. To hold him closer. To keep him exactly in place, where they could both hide. Together.

As long as no one turned on the light.

It was sort of like a hug, no matter how she told herself silently, over and over, that it was *not* a hug. It was a hold. It was for their safety and their protection that she had her arm snug around his waist.

If they were somewhere else—just about anywhere—it might look like they were dancing. Slow dancing.

She wanted to laugh at the absurdity of it all, so she forced herself to swallow. To focus on the danger lurking outside that door. Not how tall and sturdy he seemed, like she could lean her cheek against his chest and be perfectly safe.

She knew better than that. No one could keep her safe, not even herself.

In the quiet of only their careful breathing and beating hearts, she heard the slight jiggle of the doorknob. As if someone had tried it and, finding it locked, given up.

Please give up and go away. Please. Please. Please.

She didn't say anything and neither did Landon. He kept his free hand straight at his side, didn't make any attempt to touch her the way she was touching him. Almost like he was keeping that hand free to be ready to fight.

But the door never opened. Time stretched on and on and on and nothing happened. Except she could hear the easy, steady beat of Landon's heart as he stood perfectly still with her.

Landon began easing away, and gave her hand one last squeeze before he disentangled himself. "Stay right here. I'm just going to make sure they're gone."

"But—"

She hadn't even gotten the full word out before he'd slid out of the office, leaving her in the dark, completely unsure what to do. Follow him? Follow his instructions and stay put? She didn't fully understand what had just happened.

Clearly someone had been in the fort with them, but they hadn't tried to get past the locked door to Mr. Field's office. Would it have been a police officer checking up on the crime scene? Were they about to be caught and arrested?

Hazeleigh closed her eyes and took a careful breath. She'd have to find a way to get Landon out of it. Claim that she'd…forced him to help her.

Like anyone is going to believe you forced him to do anything.

Still, she'd try. She couldn't stand the idea of him getting into trouble for her. She hadn't wanted him to help her in the first place. She should be halfway to Nebraska by now, but instead he'd stopped her. Tried to help.

Why couldn't he have just listened and let her handle this? Why couldn't he have just…?

Oh, she didn't know. She only knew the idea of him being in trouble because of her made her sick to her stomach. She didn't want to be anyone's burden, anyone's blame. Ever since Amberleigh had disappeared ten years ago, Dad had blamed her. Before that, he'd never come out and said it, but she'd always thought he'd somehow blamed her for Mom's death, too.

Hazeleigh shook her head. This had nothing to do with Dad. Or even blame and bad feelings. It had to do with…Mr. Field. He was dead. For some random missing files?

None of it added up.

Landon returned and she figured his flashlight being on was a good sign they were alone again.

"Whoever it was is gone. And we need to get gone, too."

"You don't think it was the police?"

"No."

Hazeleigh's anxiety changed—from worry over Landon getting into trouble, to worry over who on earth was also sneaking around the fort in the middle of the night. "Then who?"

"I don't know, but we're going to find out." He grabbed her hand—no gentle offering this time. He began to pull her out of the office, then hurriedly locked it from the inside and shut the door.

"How are we going to find out?" Hazeleigh asked as he all but dragged her through the front room and toward the door through which they'd entered. It was open, but she was almost certain they'd closed it behind them.

But Landon didn't seem to care about that. He slid out the door, pulling her behind them. He left it open as he led her back toward the horses.

"You know the way back to the schoolhouse," he said sternly. "Go there and—"

"What are you going to do?"

"I'm going to track whoever was in here. We have to know who if we're going to figure out why."

Hazeleigh pulled her hand out of his, though it was a bit of a struggle to get her hand free. But no, that wasn't how this was going to go. She stopped in her tracks. "No. Not without me, you aren't."

THERE WAS NO time to waste. Landon had already given the intruder too much of a head start for his liking, but for Hazeleigh's sake he'd had to wait and really make sure the intruder was gone.

Who would it have been? Certainly not a cop. A cop would have unlocked the door. And wouldn't have been sneaking around in the dark, even if he'd suspected someone had broken in.

Who else would be sneaking around in the middle of the night, trying to get into the office? To Landon, the only sensible answer was the actual murderer.

He couldn't just let him get away.

"No?" he said carefully to Hazeleigh. Maybe she'd hear how ridiculous that *no* was if he said it back to her.

"You can't just…send me away. I have to go with you."

"I know how to track someone, Hazeleigh. And what to do if I'm caught. We don't even know who we're dealing with."

"You said I was a part of this."

"You're the center of this." He had to fight the frustration rising inside of him. He didn't want to snap at her. She'd likely flinch and do that thing that was far too close to a cower for his tastes, which would make him feel like he'd kicked a puppy when all he was trying to do was *help*. "But I'm the one who knows how to handle things like this."

"How would you know that?"

"Why are you so full of questions now? Why can't you listen so I can get you out of this mess?" He regretted the words, and the snap in his voice, almost instantaneously.

But she didn't flinch or cower. She stood very still. When she spoke, her words were steady. And accusatory. "You said I was going to fight for myself, Landon. You said that. Because I wanted to do this on my own, and—"

"You wanted to run away," he corrected, as softly as possible.

"I still do. I don't want to worry the police will connect you to this. I don't want to worry that I'll be the reason you—"

"Stop," he said, and he did his best to keep his emotions tethered, but it was a tough thing to do, and his words came out clipped. "Let's be clear. This is my choice. My choice to get involved, to help, to break into the fort. More than yours, in fact. You're not the *reason* I'll get in trouble. I am. And whoever started this whole thing by killing an innocent man."

She remained very still, and he couldn't read the exact change of her expression with only the light from the moon and stars to illuminate her. "But…" She couldn't seem to come up with anything to refute his statements.

"No *buts*. Now, time is wasting. I know what I'm doing. I can do this. But I need to know you'll go back to the schoolhouse and hide while I do it." He'd need daylight now. At least a little of it.

"You're going to track him. And then what?"

"See who he is."

"And then what?"

"It'll depend on a lot of factors. Identifying him is the first and most important step. I'll wait right here while you get across the highway. Then I'll follow the tracks once I get some daylight."

"How do you know there are tracks?"

"I saw a few. Heading south behind the fort."

She seemed to mull over his plan, then shook her head. She untangled Buttercup's reins and began to mount her horse. "We don't need to wait for daylight," she said, swinging into the saddle.

Landon could only stare up at her. "Huh?"

"I have an idea where he's going."

"How?"

"Pretty much the only reason to go that way is to get to Mr. Field's house."

Landon didn't have a clue where Mr. Field lived. He was reasonably sure with some daylight he could track the intruder. Even more certain that if Hazeleigh gave him directions right now, he'd be able to find it in the dark.

But she wasn't taking no for an answer. And she knew the way, so there'd be no mistakes. She wanted to fight, and in the strangest way it was progress for her. Good for her.

Why did it have to be now, when he wanted to pack her off and hide her away, and handle the situation without putting her in danger?

Landon sighed and got up on his horse. "All right. We'll do this together, but I'm in charge."

She stared at him for a moment or two, solemn and serious. "Of course you are."

And though she said it as though she meant it, Landon had the sneaking suspicion they were both very, very wrong.

Chapter Eight

Hazeleigh urged Buttercup forward. She had no idea why. The sensible thing would be to go hide in the schoolhouse and let Landon handle this. He knew what he was doing. He'd said so himself.

She didn't quite know what that meant, but she believed him. Landon seemed endlessly capable of just about anything.

But she knew how to find Mr. Field's house in the dark. She knew what to look for…sort of. Maybe.

It just felt like a thing she needed to do. If she wasn't going to run, how could she just sit around and wait for someone else to clean up the mess? Someone who might get in trouble on her behalf.

She just…couldn't.

"Not too fast," Landon cautioned. "Whoever it was had a head start, and even if the only sensible location they're headed to is Mr. Field's house, we still don't know who or why."

"What *do* we know, Landon?" she asked, slowing Buttercup's pace. It felt like a crawl. She knew it wasn't fair to be grumpy with him, and he was probably right about the don't-go-galloping-into-danger thing. But she was tired, and she wanted this whole mystery *over*.

"We know someone—who wasn't the cops—came lurking about the fort tonight."

"And gave up when the door was locked. Some crazed murderer."

Landon was quiet for a long time before he spoke, and when he did, it was in a grave tone. "It doesn't take a crazed, unpredictable person to kill, Hazeleigh. That's the problem. Someone called the police when you left the fort. There's premeditation written all over this. From Mr. Field's death, to you finding him, to someone calling the police on *you*." He was quiet for a few moments. "It has to connect to the work. If there are files missing, and he was killed in his office… Tell me more about Mr. Field's research and what files were missing from his office."

"He wanted to find the gold that disappeared in this supposed bank robbery. But that's the problem—most historians agree the bank robbery never took place, that it was just a myth. A lot of locals believe it was all a ruse to keep the railroad and the land speculators out—make them think it was too dangerous. That's also why they named the town Wilde."

"Didn't most towns back then want railroads and land speculators?"

"Towns, yes. Ranchers, no. Bent was close enough for railroads, without being close enough for people to start encroaching on pasture."

"If there's no evidence it happened, why was Mr. Field dedicating his life to studying it?"

"He believed. I love history as much as the next person. No, that isn't true. I love history *more* than the next person. And there have been times I got caught up in Mr. Field's enthusiasm and thought he might be right, but at the end of the day, it's…lore, and he *wanted* to believe more than he had evidence to believe."

Historical research was supposed to be about facts, not feelings. Not hopes and maybes. Dates, artifacts, first-hand accounts. Not fanciful dreams of bank robbers and *gold* that might still be around today. But more often that not, she'd *wanted* Mr. Field to be right, more than she'd ever actually believed he was. "He's been doing the same research for decades. He's never found anything that'd be enough to kill over."

Landon sighed, and the sound was sad. Sad enough that she looked over at him, and though she could just make out his profile in the moonlight, she had the aching wish she could comfort him somehow.

"You'd be surprised what people are willing to kill over, Hazeleigh."

"That sounds like you have personal experience."

He shook his head in the dim light but didn't refute her statement. He didn't explain his experience either. Hazeleigh found it odd that she wanted to press, because she wanted to *know*, when usually she much preferred keeping to herself.

But Mr. Field's cabin was just up ahead. "Not much farther now. If this person was heading there, should we stop now and walk, like we did at the fort?"

"Yes," Landon said. "Is there any cover around the house?"

Cover. Such a strange word for places to hide. It made her wonder what Landon's life was like before he and his brothers moved here. But now was not the time for wondering or questions. "Not really in the front. It's just a little cabin in the middle of a stretch of land. There's a creek that runs through his backyard and there are a few heritage birches."

"Heritage birches?"

"Trees."

"You know the types of trees?"

He sounded a little *too* amused for her tastes. "I know lots of things, Landon."

He chuckled. "I know you do."

She wanted to take offense, to feel like he was laughing at her. He had to be, didn't he? But it didn't *sound* mean. It didn't *feel* mean, the way so many men in her life had been.

She let out a long breath. Landon wasn't her father, or Douglas, or even Kenny, her high-school boyfriend. But the fact of the matter was, she did like Landon, so surely *something* about him had to be suspect. Right?

None of that mattered now though. She thought about the layout of Mr. Field's land and cabin. "Follow me."

He did without question, or trying to make her feel like she didn't know what she was doing. She kept waiting for a complaint or one of those snide questions disguised as concern that she was so used to from the men she'd let into her life.

He simply followed.

It was such a confusing feeling Hazeleigh *had* to focus only on where they were going, or she might second-guess herself and even she knew in this moment there was no time for that.

She gave the cabin a wide berth and led them around to the back of the Field property. They couldn't get too far from the cabin in the back without crossing the creek. The horses would probably be fine, but Hazeleigh would want more daylight for the horses to make the crossing.

"Here," she said. It was far enough away from the cabin that even if it was daylight, the horses wouldn't be visible in this cluster of trees, which also gave them a place to tie the horses.

Landon would have to take them back to the ranch soon. Not only did they need to be fed and watered, but also if daylight dawned and two horses were missing, his brothers and Zara were bound to know he was out helping her.

"We can't take too much time," she said.

"Yeah, but we can't let this opportunity pass."

Hazeleigh wasn't so sure about that, but she got off Buttercup and tied the reins to the tree while Landon did the same with his horse.

"Okay, they're good. Lead the way."

It was even stranger having someone tell her to *lead*, but she was the expert here. She had to remember that. They also needed to stick close to one another, and until the cabin came into view and Landon knew the target, they needed to…

Well, like they'd done back at the fort. She held out her hand. She couldn't read Landon's expression in the dark, but it felt like there was a slight hesitation…just like her own not so long ago.

But before she had time to process it, to try and understand his hesitation, his big hand gripped hers.

The touch affected her. She couldn't deny that. His

hand was warm and calloused and *big*, and it felt safe. She should know better than to feel safe, but she couldn't fight the warmth that moved through her.

She could ignore it though. She could move forward without *dwelling* on it. She led him over the soft swells of land. The moon was beginning to fade, the stars giving way to a lighter sky. This was taking too long, but…

The cabin was right there. It was still shrouded in darkness, and she couldn't make out anything that might give away someone sneaking around.

"Let's stay in the trees as we get closer," Landon said quietly.

The brush wasn't exactly full cover. There were spaces to walk through between some of the trees, but she hoped the dark hid their moving shadows. She held Landon's hand and drew him closer and closer to the cabin.

"There," Landon said, pulling her to a stop and pointing at…something.

Hazeleigh didn't see anything. It all looked dark to her, but she believed he'd seen something. She had no doubt that Landon knew what he was doing.

"What do we do now?" she asked in a whisper.

"You'll wait here."

"Landon."

"Behind a tree. Out of sight." He dropped her hand and began to step away from the trees. "Stay—" With no warning, Landon lunged, grabbed her hard and jerked her behind the narrow bark of one of the trees.

Almost at the exact same time, a gunshot rang out in the dark.

IT WAS CLOSE. Too close. Landon figured the only thing that saved them was the dark. The sting on his shoulder was little more than a graze, and he was damn lucky for that.

He knew Hazeleigh wouldn't see it that way. But that wasn't important now. What was important was finding cover.

"We have to get you out of here."

"Me?" she all but shrieked. "Us," she hissed.

Another shot. Hazeleigh winced and grabbed on to him. Landon tried to survey where the shot was coming from. He'd seen a silhouette *inside* the house, but it couldn't be whoever was shooting at them…unless the shooter had a window open.

Possible. Far too many possibilities.

Landon stilled, pushed Hazeleigh out of his mind and listened. He'd been here too many times to count. Shot at. Waiting. Planning. He knew how to do this. He knew how to protect his team.

But Hazeleigh wasn't part of an elite military team. She was a civilian. This wasn't the Middle East and he wasn't in tactical gear and…

He blew out a slow breath, finding that old center of calm. He pushed away all the worries, concerns and possibilities, and focused on the *now*.

A cold ball of fear pitted in his stomach. Footsteps. Coming for them. He grabbed Hazeleigh's hand again and began to lead her away. He had to get her somewhere safe.

They couldn't run for the horses when he didn't know how many people were here. What kind of guns they had. But if they took a roundabout run back to the horses, maybe they could lose whoever was after them.

The biggest problem was that the shooter seemed to have something that allowed him to see in the dark.

So Landon stuck to the trees. He didn't exactly know where he was going. Cover was more important than where they ended up for right now. Moving quickly and as soundlessly as possible—something Hazeleigh was surprisingly good at—was all that mattered.

He thought they were making headway. There hadn't been any more gunshots, and when they paused to take a breath, there were no more footsteps.

"If we cross the creek here, we can get more tree cover and then double back to the horses," Hazeleigh said. "I don't know if that's a good idea, I just—"

"It's perfect." Another shot rang out and Hazeleigh jolted, but Landon held her hand tightly. "Farther away. Wrong direction. Whatever our shooter is following, he lost us. So let's get even more lost."

"It'll be slick. Especially in the dark. Rocks can seem sturdy and then move on you. It'll be shockingly cold. So brace yourself."

He wanted to laugh. It was downright sweet of her, trying to warn him. She had no idea what he'd done, seen, endured. And it felt…a little too nice for someone to worry over him like he was just your average civilian.

"Yes, ma'am," he murmured, trying to make sure neither his amusement nor the way her concern touched him came through in his voice.

Hazeleigh pulled him a few more steps. He could hear the gurgling, the rush of water over rocks. Some worry slid under all that good feeling. "That sounds like something a hell of a lot bigger than a creek."

"It isn't deep, but it'll be icy. It'd be tough to cross in the daylight. In the dark, it's downright dangerous. But…"

Yeah, *but*. He looked around. The dark was getting lighter all the time, even if the sun hadn't fully risen yet. Still, his flashlight would give them away. Hopefully the roar of the rushing creek would hide the sound of them trying to cross it.

He squeezed Hazeleigh's hand. "Well, hold on." He inched forward, toward the creek. The bank was steep and that made things difficult. When his boot touched water, he had to fight the urge to pull back. March in Wyoming wasn't exactly *spring* and getting wet didn't hold any appeal.

But they had to get out of here. Resolutely, he stepped into the water. He bit back a string of curses. Holy *hell* it was cold. But the icy bite of the water only came up to about mid-calf. Once his feet were steady, grounded on two solid rocks, he looked back at Hazeleigh.

"Get on my back."

"What?"

"You're going to put your arms on my shoulders, your legs around my waist, and we'll get across that way."

"Don't be—"

"We don't have time to argue. Just do it."

The stern tone must have caught her off guard enough that she didn't argue and followed his order. From the taller part of the bank, she braced her hands on his shoulders, wrapped one leg around his left side. He gripped it. She gave a little hop and he managed to grab her other leg.

Then he began to walk. It was much harder with the added weight, but he'd endured worse. Heavier loads. More difficult challenges. And he thought about all of those challenges, rather than her pressed up against his back, or his arms hooked under her knees. He thought about the desert in the midafternoon rather than the stabbing frigid ice swirling around his legs.

He got about halfway across before another gunshot sounded. Much closer now, as if the gunman had figured out where they were. Hazeleigh jerked, but he managed to keep his balance. But the gunshot was too close.

There was only one option, no matter how much Landon hated it. "You're going to have to get down." He crouched and lowered her into the icy water, holding her and giving her as much of a steady hand as he could so she didn't fall.

She hissed out a breath as her feet came down, but she didn't complain. Water splashed around their legs, no doubt soaking her skirt. They had to get out of the water.

"I'm going to let go of your hand," he said as quietly as he could over the rush of the water. "When I do, go. Crawl out. Run. Just run. Zigzag pattern, just in case. Head for whatever cover you can find."

"But—"

"No *buts*. I'll be right behind you." He gave her hand one last reassuring squeeze, then let go. "Now!"

She scrambled away, a little more noisily than he'd have liked. But she followed his instructions, and he hadn't lied—he was right behind her. He gave her a boost out of the water on the other side of the creek.

"Go," he hissed when she hesitated. Then she did. He could see her move in a zigzag pattern, no doubt slowed down by her sodden skirt. He hefted himself out of the creek with one arm, dragging a decent-size rock out of the water with the other. He heaved it as far down the creek in the opposite direction as he could.

When another gunshot rang out, he hit the deck, but he was pretty sure it had been aimed in the direction of the big splash he'd made with the rock. He kept moving, crawling forward on the ground, until he caught up with Hazeleigh.

She was also on her hands and knees. He grabbed her hand. "Come on. Fast as you can."

They got to their feet and ran. He hoped to God they were going in the direction of the horses.

When Hazeleigh gave his hand a little yank, he changed course, trusting her to know where to take them.

When they reached the horses, he nearly shouted out a hallelujah. The sun was beginning to peek over the swell of land to the east. "No time to waste."

She nodded and they both got into their saddles.

"I'll follow you."

She nodded again. It concerned him that she wasn't saying anything, but then she was off, and he could only urge his horse to follow.

Chapter Nine

Hazeleigh thought she might pass out. Her body was shivering so hard it was almost impossible to hold on to the reins. But she had to get Landon back to the schoolhouse.

With the sun rising, she knew they had to get far away from Mr. Field's, but it also freed her to urge her horse into a run rather than the careful pace of a night ride.

She didn't hear another gunshot. She knew that didn't mean they were out of danger, but it allowed her to *think* a little.

Back to the schoolhouse. Then what? She didn't know. What had they figured out? As far as she could tell, a fat lot of nothing. And she might have gotten herself hypothermia for the trouble.

They rode and rode for what seemed like forever. She nearly sobbed in relief when she saw the schoolhouse come into view. The sun was fully rising now, a pretty pale orange and pink. Landon had to get back to the house. Someone would know he was gone, that he'd taken two horses. She glanced at him, riding right next to her. Wet and bedraggled.

No, he couldn't exactly go straight to the house either.

She urged Buttercup to go faster, and they made it to the schoolhouse quickly. They dismounted and her legs almost gave out she was shaking so hard, but she managed to grab onto the stirrup and hold herself up.

Landon cursed, his hands immediately going to her arms and beginning to rub up and down. "We've got to get you some dry clothes."

"I'm o-k-k-ay," she said, her teeth chattering in direct contrast to her words. "The sun will d-d-dry me r-r-right up. Wh-what about you?"

"I'm fine." He sounded very firm and sure, but she didn't believe him. He looked around, then shook his head. "Take off what you can."

She blinked at him. Surely he didn't mean…

"I know we don't have anything dry to change into, but if we can get some of the excess water off our clothes, it'll help."

He wanted her to take her clothes off. In front of him. She could only gape.

Something in his expression changed. She didn't know what, but it got a little harder. Then he pulled off his sweatshirt. Underneath, the T-shirt he wore was wet and plastered to his skin, outlining every ridge and every muscle. She made an involuntary noise that she hoped he didn't hear.

He wrung out his sweatshirt and an entire stream of water dripped onto the ground. "See? Just wring the water out. Damp isn't great, but it's better than soaking."

She swallowed. Her mouth felt like dust. *You are an imbecile*, she told herself harshly.

He shook his head when she still didn't move. "Tell you what," he said gently. "You step inside. Take things off, one at a time, hand them to me, I'll wring them out, then hand them back to you. I'm not looking to be a peeping Tom, Hazeleigh."

"Of course not," she said. What little heat she had left in her body seemed to rush for her cheeks. She hadn't even considered he might want to *see* something. She remembered him smiling when he'd made that comment about being *sweet on you* and honestly, the cold had gone to her brain.

"Y-you need to get b-b-back."

"I'll handle it." He kept rubbing his big hands up and down her arms, but they were covered in the thick, wet sweater and even the friction didn't do much. "I promise. If I have to lie through my teeth, no one's going to know I know where you are, okay? I promise."

And she wasn't sure she'd ever believed anyone's promise as wholeheartedly as she believed his. Which she knew was a problem, but she was shivering too hard to care.

"Go on now," he said firmly with a last squeeze of her arms. "Or I'm going to end up having to take you to the hospital, because I will hide you through a lot of things, Hazeleigh, but I'm not about to let you freeze to death just to avoid a false accusation against you."

She swallowed and then managed to move away. She opened the door and stepped into the dark of the schoolhouse. It was *almost* warmer inside. She sucked in a breath and peeled off the heavy, dripping sweater. Even the wind of the horse ride hadn't done much to get rid of the water.

She looked at the gap in the door. Landon's hand was just…there, patiently waiting for her shirt so he could wring the water onto the ground outside.

She handed him her sweater through the gap in the door. "Do the outer layer first," he instructed. "Then switch, all right? So get the skirt and whatever was under the sweater off. I'll try to get the sun to warm them up a little, then we'll switch."

Switch. Like her *underwear*. In his *hands*. She didn't know what to do with that, but when his hand reappeared in the gap, she knew she had to take off her skirt and hand it to him.

His hand disappeared for a few minutes and Hazeleigh pulled the camisole off so that she was only in her bra and the slip shorts she wore under her skirts. She looked at the quickly dawning day through the crack in the door.

She was cold and miserable and on the run, but her heart felt…oddly bruised by Landon making promises to her when he didn't have to. He'd been shot at because of *her* and he just kept moving forward like it was all par for the course.

Like it didn't bother him at all that they'd gone to the fort, and to Mr. Field's house, and found more questions than answers.

The door moved, the gap getting a little bigger as he shoved his hand in again. But she was looking, and she could see him now.

He was standing there in his boxers, not looking at all as if he was shivering like she was. But that wasn't what caught her attention, or not only that. "Landon…" And she forgot she was in just her bra and the shorts.

She stepped through the crack and reached out to touch the long, deep scar that went from shoulder to hip. It was a jagged line, and though it had clearly been there for a very long time, the mark was so clear against the marble of his skin, it nearly took her breath away.

She didn't know *why* she felt compelled to touch it, or why her heart ached when she did. It was just…instinct. Coming from that same place inside of her that her bad feelings usually came from.

But reality eventually crashed in, reminding her she was touching his abs. And they were *abs*. All of him was pure muscle, and while she'd always figured he was well built under layers of winter clothes, she hadn't had a *clue* he might look like a movie superhero underneath all that.

Or that it might jangle around inside of her, making her forget everything including propriety. And some kind of *consent*.

She jerked back like she'd been scalded. And maybe she had. Or maybe she had hypothermia of the *brain*. "I'm sorry."

He shrugged easily. "It's a shocking scar."

"How…? No, I'm sorry, it's none of my business."

"Doesn't mean you can't ask."

She finally looked up from the scar. His mouth was curved in a kind of amused line, but it wasn't a smile. And his eyes were sad. She wanted to step forward and hug him. He looked like he needed a hug.

He also looked like he'd be warm.

The weak morning sunlight was shining on them now, but it didn't really offer any warmth. She was pretty sure any warmth she felt was a figment of her imagination, or maybe embarrassment powering her from the inside out.

Then she noticed the little trail of red on his arm. An arm he was angling away from her. Quite purposefully, now that she was paying attention.

"You're bleeding."

"It's nothing," he said, even offering a smile. "The important thing is—"

He was angling it even more away from her, which made her reach out and grab him to keep him in place. She moved around him. The bleeding was hardly *nothing*.

"How did that happen?"

He tried to pull away, but she held firm. She tried to think of anything she might have in the schoolhouse to patch him up. "You need it cleaned out. You need a bandage."

"We have a lot bigger problems than a scratch. You need to focus."

"I am focusing! You're *hurt*." And it was because of her. "A scratch," she scoffed. "What macho nonsense is that? The only way you could have gotten that deep of a cut is if…" She stopped, felt the heat rush out of her and the chilled shaking start again. He'd been *shot*.

"I'm *fine*." He pointed to his scar. "I've been seriously injured before, Hazeleigh. I know what it's like. This? It's nothing."

"It's something to me."

His sharp inhale kept her from saying anything else or moving forward to see what she could do about the cut—which made her feel a little woozy if she looked too closely at it. But Landon looked at her like she'd impaled him because she cared that he was hurt *because of her.*

"Lan—"

She couldn't complete his name, which was fine enough, because she didn't have an earthly clue what she was going to say, only that the moment seemed to call for *something.*

But he put his hand on her face. It was gentle and it was sweet, and she might not understand the emotion moving through him, but she saw it on his face.

And she wanted to lean into it. No matter how cold or scared or mixed up she was. *This* was warm and real and good. And there wasn't one bad feeling or red flag here.

"That's very sweet," he said, his voice soft. His hand was still on her face and his gaze was…everywhere. Like he was memorizing her face.

She found herself returning the favor, or maybe she was just looking for a road map. A way forward.

"But I've laid my life on the line for a lot less. This is just a scratch." With his free hand, he pointed to the scar across his chest. "My father did this to me in a drunken rage. He wasn't sorry. He didn't feel any kind of responsibility. It was the whiskey's fault, in his mind. So I appreciate that you're trying to take some kind of blame here, but it isn't yours. I understand blame. I understand the weight of injuries you go into with your eyes wide open. I know what I'm risking here, Hazeleigh, and I don't mind risking it for you. So I need you to stop blaming yourself for anything that happens in the course of trying to prove you're innocent. Helping you is an honorable task that I'm taking with my eyes wide open."

The lump in her throat grew with intensity. She knew—just knew—he didn't want her tears for *him*, but she knew…

His father's *physical* abuse was not the same as her father's emotional abuse. A clear fact with all these marks on. It wasn't the same, but she understood. The difference in choosing something and having it happen to you. When you chose things that might end in being hurt, it didn't feel so bad because at least it wasn't your parent inflicting the harm.

"We've got a long way to go on this," he continued in that same soft, earnest voice that she'd never once heard come out of him. There was no smile, no joke. Just honesty. "So let's agree on this right here, right now. Everything from this point on? A choice. Eyes wide open. No guilt."

"But I'm so good at guilt."

He laughed and flashed that lightning-quick grin that made her knees weak. Or maybe it was the cold and the shivering. "Yeah, you are," he agreed. "But you're going to have to let that go." His smile faded, the blue of his eyes seeming to deepen. "For me."

HAZELEIGH WAS LOOKING at him, eyes so wide she might as well be a Disney princess. Her hand had drifted back down to his scar, and he didn't know how it could feel like some kind of healing. She could hardly make it go away, hardly make him forgive his father for those hellish years.

But she'd taken…the weight of it, somehow. He'd

been injured before. He'd carried his brothers on his back and known they'd do the same—that was a kind of care deeper than any blood tie because they'd been through hell together, trusted each other through hell.

But it wasn't the same as Hazeleigh… He didn't even know how to explain it. Only that her compassion or empathy undid him.

Not the time or place. And Hazeleigh was stronger than she gave herself credit for, but he should be more careful with her. She'd been through a lot, and this was far from over.

He cleared his throat and took a step back. "You're going to get hypothermia." The words came out clipped, and both confusion and hurt registered on her face before she smoothed it out. "Your clothes won't be dry, but if you take off the—" he had to clear his throat again "—wet underthings and put the sweater and skirt back on until they dry a little, you should be okay until I can come back with some dry things for you."

She nodded carefully. Then squinted at the horses. "How are you going to explain two horses missing?"

"I'm not. I'm leaving Buttercup with you." He had to get away. He had to…act. He moved to the clothes he'd spread outside and began to pull them back on. He hadn't had a chance to ring out his boxers, and the sun had done very little to dry his socks or jeans, but he'd be back to the ranch soon enough.

She was the one to be worried about. He got dressed, then gathered her things and handed them to her. "You switch out those clothes. I'll be back with food and dry clothes soon as I can." He didn't make eye contact.

Not because he was embarrassed. It wasn't even

self-preservation. If he looked at her, he wouldn't go. And if he didn't go…

Well, he had to get moving. The end.

He stalked toward the horse, trying to untangle his brain. He had Hazeleigh's list in his pocket, water-logged maybe, but hopefully intact. Either way, he'd hack into the police server and find some new information. Maybe figure out a way to make an anonymous tip about someone shooting near Mr. Field's house. Maybe the police would be smart enough to realize Hazeleigh didn't have a gun, so it couldn't have been her.

Before he could fully untether his horse from where he'd been tied, Hazeleigh stopped him with her hands, taking his in hers. He knew he shouldn't, but he couldn't stop himself. He looked down at her.

She looked pretty and he kept his eyes on hers, because if he looked lower and took in that expanse of pale, freckled skin…

"Get your arm looked at," she said. Insisted, maybe. "Please. If you have to out me, that's fine. The most important thing is that you're okay."

He looked into her dark eyes and he could barely think through the driving desire to kiss her. Just once. Just to get a taste.

"I'm not going to out you," he finally said, hoping it didn't sound as strangled as he felt. "But I promise, I'll get it patched up before I come back."

She squeezed his hands and smiled up at him. "Thank you."

He gave her a stiff nod and got up on the horse, having to shift and adjust a few times to find a comfortable sitting position. "For the love of God, get yourself dressed, Hazeleigh. A man can only take so much," he muttered, and then urged his horse into a run.

Away from her. Away from desire. And toward responsibility. He wondered when he'd gotten so damn straight and narrow.

Chapter Ten

A man can only take so much.

Hazeleigh had stood there for probably too long looking down at herself. The bra was a serviceable cotton one. The shorts were functional. She couldn't really imagine she looked *alluring* even in her underwear. Her hair had to be a mess and her makeup from *yesterday* was long gone. She was a shivering mess.

Douglas had once refused to take her to a concert they'd bought tickets to because she'd been too *shabby*-looking, and that had been right after she'd spent almost an hour getting ready. Kenny had often complained bitterly about everything to do with her appearance, after he'd gotten what he wanted from her.

It had been a whole thing, and once she'd gotten herself out of it, she'd seen it for what it was. A kind of…self-punishment. Because while she resolutely told herself Amberleigh's disappearance hadn't been her fault, sometimes she'd agreed with her father.

Why hadn't she had any of her bad feelings that might have predicted Amberleigh's runaway attempt? Amberleigh wasn't just her sister, they were *triplets*. Hazeleigh should have felt it, she should have known.

Hazeleigh blew out a breath and did what Landon had instructed. *Focus*. Her misguided assessment of male partners and self-punishment was not on the table. She had to avoid hypothermia at this point. She had to figure out who...

Someone had *shot* at them. One of the bullets had grazed Landon's arm. It made her stomach churn even now.

He'd told her to stop blaming herself and as much as she wanted to take offense, how could she? It was the truth. She did, in fact, do that, and it made things harder.

Still, it wasn't easy to just *accept* he might get hurt or be in trouble on account of her. When she was...

She closed her eyes and walked into the schoolhouse. She would change out of her underwear, into the damp but not sopping-wet outer clothes, and she would deal with what she could.

She'd spent too long letting herself feel like her father wanted her to feel. A failure. Worthless. It had taken some hard times, and eventually talking to a counselor, to start climbing out of that self-destructive behavior.

She had every right to fight for her innocence here, and if Landon chose to fight alongside her—as he was insistent on doing—then it wasn't about what she deserved or not.

Sometimes, people wanted to help. Zara had always been there. Of course, that was about love and family, and Landon wasn't family.

Hazeleigh paused for a moment, completely naked and frozen to the bone in the old, crumbling schoolhouse, and heard Landon's voice in her head. *A man can only take so much.* What would it have been like to tell him he didn't have to *take* it? What would it be like to…believe someone could love and be there for her by *choice*? Not because of family ties.

Love. She had a long way to go before she could worry about being in love with *anyone*, and it seemed wholly inconceivable to imagine a man like Landon ever being in love with her. So it was quite foolish to stand here and daydream. She pulled on the sweater, shivering anew because though it might not be *as* wet, the sun hadn't been enough to really warm the material.

She'd hang her underwear somewhere out in the sun. See what she could do to feed and water Buttercup. Maybe brush her down. And she would think about the files missing from Mr. Field's filing cabinet and try to find some kind of clue. Pattern. *Something* that might hint at who had killed him.

She would be productive. Proactive. For Mr. Field. For herself. And she wouldn't let herself think about *love* or scars or the way Landon's hand had fitted against her cheek at *all*.

But as she turned for the bag she'd packed and the bag Landon had left last night, she frowned. Something…wasn't right.

Hadn't she very carefully put her bag up on the little shelf in what had once been a closet that no longer had a door? And Landon had hung his up on the hook in the back, rusted and ancient but still there screwed into the plaster.

Now, both sat by the door, open.

Hazeleigh hesitated then reached out for hers. She

wanted it to be an animal. Bear. Giant raccoon. Something that had grabbed their bags and moved them in search of food. It *could* be.

But she didn't know any wild animal that would take the bags to the same spot and leave them leaning against each other by the door.

Anxiety arced through her, but she opened her bag as far as it would go. Everything appeared to still be in there, but it was… She was almost certain it had been upended and then repacked.

She hesitated in touching anything, but there was no bad feeling. No inner signal of danger. It wasn't a foolproof system, but she couldn't just…ignore the bag.

She pulled out the scarf she'd forgotten she'd packed and wrapped it around her neck, willing herself to think clearly. Someone had been in here and gone through her things. She pulled out every item carefully. The only thing missing was the cash she'd had in the front pocket, but the other stack of bills she kept hidden in her planner was still there.

It could have just been a random passerby who had glanced through, seen some cash and taken it. She *hoped* for that.

She grabbed Landon's bag next. She didn't know everything he'd packed, but it seemed lighter than it should have. It had seemed pretty stuffed when he'd put it down yesterday. Someone had taken something he'd brought, she was almost sure of it, and it wouldn't have been cash.

She stood, looked around the room. Someone had been in here. Long gone before she and Landon arrived? Or had they seen them coming and bolted?

But who else would be using this as a hiding spot? Who else would be sneaking around and running away? And if someone was following her, why not approach her?

Or would they have seen her coming and left to call the cops and turn her in?

The cops.

She sucked in a breath. If someone knew she was here, the police might know, too. And all this running away would make her seem so much more guilty than she was.

No. It wasn't going to go down like that. And she was hardly going to sit here, waiting to get caught. She couldn't.

She grabbed both bags, stuffed her wet underwear into one of them and then went back outside. She looked around her, heart beating too hard. People could be watching. The cops could be coming.

She had to find somewhere to hide. She'd…run. Like she'd always planned. Landon might be a little put off, but—

Buttercup whinnied.

Hazeleigh stopped. Landon's voice repeated in her head. *Focus.*

Not panic. Focus.

She couldn't abandon her horse, and maybe that was a good reminder that she could hardly abandon the man who'd been *shot* because of her.

She had to swallow at the bubbling fear that Landon would suffer so much more before this was all done. But it wasn't the real kind of fear, the bone-deep bad feeling. It was panic, plain and simple.

Focus.

She looked at the vast countryside around her. The sunrise had blossomed into a sunny morning with nothing but blue sky. There weren't a lot of places to hide, and she could hardly fight the cops. She wouldn't abandon Landon, but she had to find a way to protect herself.

"All right, Buttercup," she murmured, approaching the horse, letting the steady rise and fall of her body calm her. "Let's figure something out." Something smart. Something right.

LANDON THOUGHT UP a million excuses on his way back to the house. He thought about forgoing stabling his horse and just sneaking somewhere to pretend like he'd been around all night and up early this morning. Holed up with his computer, hacking into things.

It wouldn't explain the damp state of his clothes. Or the gunshot wound on his arm.

So he'd have to do what he'd told Hazeleigh he would. Tell as much of the truth as he could without admitting he knew anything about where Hazeleigh was or that she'd been involved.

It would still be tricky. Landon might be able to lie, but his brothers were pretty good BS detectors. In a different circumstance, he would have told them. Even in this circumstance it was hard not to, because he didn't think they'd be exactly…disapproving of his actions.

It was the Hazeleigh factor that complicated things. That Jake was in love with her sister, and if Jake knew Landon knew where Hazeleigh was, Zara would know.

And Zara just…wasn't one for subtlety or sitting back and letting anyone take care of things.

Maybe that wouldn't be so bad, but Landon knew Hazeleigh wanted to keep Zara out of the investigation. Hell, she wanted to keep *him* out of this, and he wasn't close to her at all.

It's something to me, she'd said, so seriously, those brown eyes on his so wide and earnest. The way she'd touched his scar. It would be safer to convince himself he didn't matter to her, but she made it hard. Maybe she didn't care about him the way he was finding himself caring about her, but that didn't mean she didn't care at all.

If he was the reason Zara got mixed up in this, Hazeleigh would blame him. She might even hate him, and he couldn't stand the thought.

He stabled his horse, did his best to clean up in the rough-in bathroom in the stable. But no amount of barn cleaning could make him look like he hadn't been traipsing about the Wyoming wilderness hiding in creeks and getting shot at.

He'd have to show Dunne his arm. While it was nothing compared to a lot of the injuries he'd suffered—at home and in the army—if he went back to Hazeleigh with a little bandage slapped on it, she was going to be mad.

It's something to me.

He came out of the stable bathroom to find Cal standing at the entrance, arms folded, as if waiting.

Of course he was waiting.

"Morning, Cal," Landon offered cheerfully. With

Cal, the best bet was always to proceed as if everything was just fine.

"I don't suppose you're going to explain where you were all night? With two of our horses."

Landon did his best to look suitably confused. "Only had my horse, Cal."

Cal's mouth firmed, a clear sign he didn't believe Landon. "That doesn't explain where you were."

"Nope, sure doesn't." Landon stepped forward, smile firmly in place, but Cal blocked his exit from the stable.

Landon struggled to wrestle his temper. Temper was never the answer—especially with Cal. So he raised an eyebrow. "Do you really want to have a fight, Cal?"

"Do you?"

"I could take you, old man." He'd always loved to tease Cal about their five-year difference in age, but today it didn't come out as teasingly humorous as it should have. He needed some sleep.

And Cal was in his way. Saying nothing. Just *looking* at him with that disapproving, I-am-your-superior-officer expression.

"I don't have to answer to you anymore. That's the beauty of Team Breaker no longer existing." Landon kept his hands at his sides, though the desire to shove his way out the exit was screaming through him.

"Are you not a part of the team anymore?" Cal asked with that same maddening calm that had always made him a great leader.

But they weren't in the military anymore. They weren't Team Breaker anymore. They were brothers. Ranchers. Business partners in a way.

But they weren't a team—because there was no team. "The team doesn't exist."

"Doesn't it?"

Guilt, yeah, Cal knew how to use that, too. Landon could shove his way free. He could even have a fistfight with Cal. It'd be a toss-up who'd come out on top, and it might even feel good—pounding *or* getting pounded. A concrete thing instead of all these what-ifs in his head.

But he didn't want to fight with Cal. Fighting the people he loved only ever made him feel like his father.

So he told Cal the story. Sort of. He left out every mention of Hazeleigh. He was the one who'd gone to the fort, alone, to see if he could figure anything out. He'd noticed someone else, followed them to Mr. Field's and then been shot at and had to escape.

"And what possessed you to do all that?" Cal's voice was deceptively mild, which was the worst. Because Landon wanted to defend himself, when that would only dig him into a hole.

He needed to play it cool. "We all know Hazeleigh isn't a killer. I don't know why you'd be surprised I might try and figure out a way to prove it to the cops."

"Alone?"

"We're supposed to keep a low profile. You're always telling me that." Not that they'd done a very good job of it in the beginning. Jake and Brody had both gotten tangled in messes that had led to them getting town attention.

But nothing had come of it. Team Breaker was still in hiding. No one suspected the Thompson brothers were terrorist targets.

"You got yourself shot."

Landon scoffed and held up his arm. "We both know this is nothing."

"But the danger isn't nothing. You shouldn't be handling this alone. I get you want to help—we all want to help—but not alone. We all know teams work better."

"Sometimes you have to work alone," Landon insisted, because as much as he appreciated Cal wanting to work as a team, it was best for everyone if he was the only one who knew where Hazeleigh was.

Cal didn't respond, so Landon took the opportunity to leave. Or try to. Cal stopped him again, this time with a hand to the shoulder. Before Landon could get irritated, he said something that made no sense.

"Keep your distance from Jake best you can."

"Huh?"

"You're a horrible liar. If he suspects you know where Hazeleigh is, like *I* suspect you do considering it's her horse missing, he and Zara will be on your butt and you won't have a prayer. You want to keep this a secret? Avoid Jake."

Landon had to take a second to get his bearings. He was that transparent? Or Cal just knew him that well? Neither revelation sat particularly well with him, but he figured Cal was right.

Cal patted his shoulder then turned and walked away from the stables.

"Cal?"

Cal stopped and looked over his shoulder, and Landon grinned—not because he felt particularly *amused*, but because it was... Cal could be a cold jerk, but Landon had always known deep down it covered up the depth of what he felt. And if Landon poked at that depth, Cal really would leave him alone. "You old softy you."

Cal grunted and stormed away.

Because they weren't a *team* anymore.

They were family.

Chapter Eleven

Hazeleigh had found a place to lie in the sunshine not too far away from the schoolhouse. There was a little rock cropping, and it hid her on two sides and gave her something to lean against as she soaked in the sun.

It was still cold, so dang cold, but it was better than the dark, dank building.

Buttercup was tied to a tree, and if someone came sniffing around, she'd likely react in some way. This area was flat enough that she should be able to hear someone coming, and the area was isolated enough she doubted anyone would stumble upon her.

If someone found her, they'd really have to want to.

Her stomach trembled a little at that thought, because it was certainly possible, but this was a sensible, calm course of action. Isolated spot. Warming up and drying out her clothes. Not so far she wouldn't be able to see Landon return to the schoolhouse.

She hadn't panicked. She'd thought through her actions. Of course, she'd fallen asleep there for a little while, which wasn't smart, but here she was. Just fine.

Maybe she was still cold, and maybe she was starving and really thirsty—what little water she'd been able to collect she'd given to Buttercup—but she was okay. Everything was going to be fine.

Then she heard rustling.

Heart in her throat, she looked at Buttercup, who was happily grazing on the pasture grass—definitely not making rustling noises. Carefully, Hazeleigh got to her feet. She turned in a slow circle but saw no one.

Hazeleigh didn't have anything that could be used as a weapon. She grabbed a rock from where she'd been sitting. It was small and likely wouldn't do any damage, but it was the best she could find.

Swallowing against fear, Hazeleigh began to tiptoe toward the noise. It was probably just a squirrel. A raccoon. Maybe even a bear.

But one never knew.

She inched forward, peering through the tree branches. She thought she saw a little flash of…blue. She kept the branches between her and it, creeping around the tree. Maybe she should be running in the opposite direction. Would someone pull out a gun and kill her?

Someone had tried last night, hadn't they? Of course, that had been in the dark with her and Landon following someone.

Hazeleigh finally caught a glimpse of the blue flash for what it was.

It was…a little girl. Hazeleigh looked all around for an adult, for someone to jump out and grab her after using the girl as some kind of diversion, but there was only the little girl. Maybe about ten years old. Reddish brown hair in a flyaway-laden braid, dressed in flannel pajamas and cowboy boots.

She turned and froze when she saw Hazeleigh.

"Hello," Hazeleigh finally said, without sounding too strangled. Her heartbeat hadn't returned to normal yet, but this little girl shouldn't be out here alone. Was she lost?

The little girl just stared at her with wide hazel eyes. Some mix of fear and guilt was evident on her face.

Hazeleigh searched the area. "Are you out here alone?" she asked carefully. Maybe it was still a trap. It certainly didn't feel…right.

The girl didn't stop staring, and she didn't answer Hazeleigh's question.

"What's your name, sweetheart?"

She shook her head. "What's yours?"

Hazeleigh also wanted to shake her head, but that would be suspicious. She was certainly suspicious of this little girl. But Hazeleigh had something few people had.

A nearly identical sister. "I'm… Zara. Zara Hart." Hazeleigh forced herself to smile. "I live right over there on the Hart…well, Thompson Ranch."

"What are you doing here then?"

Now that was a question. Still, Hazeleigh kept the smile on her face. She liked kids. She'd worked at an after-school day care in high school and she knew how to deal with children. She crouched down so she was at eye level with the girl even though there was still a distance between them.

"Can I tell you a secret?"

The girl looked around, so Hazeleigh did, too. Was a parent going to come crashing through looking for their lost daughter?

But the girl's gaze came back to Hazeleigh and she shrugged. Nonchalantly, even if her eyes gleamed with interest. "Okay," the girl said.

"I like this side of the fence better. It feels…enchanted."

The little girl's eyebrows drew together. "It's just grass." She eyed Buttercup. "But I like your horse."

"Me, too. Her name's Buttercup." *And she isn't mine any longer.* "Do you want to pet her?"

There was a longing so deep in those hazel eyes that Hazeleigh wanted to step forward and give the girl a hug, but the girl shook her head. "Can't. I'm not supposed to be here."

Me either. "You don't seem lost."

"I'm not." She sighed heavily. "Is that your stuff in that old house?" the girl asked, pointing to the schoolhouse in the distance.

Hazeleigh considered. Should she admit those bags were hers? She still wasn't sure what this girl was about or where she'd come from. She hedged. "I'm not sure. What stuff are you talking about?"

The girl started walking away. Hazeleigh didn't know whether to follow or demand more answers or just let her go. It didn't make any sense.

Maybe she was delirious, and this was a hallucination. But she didn't like the idea of this girl alone in the wild, particularly with a murderer and people shooting on the loose. There weren't any livable houses on the property, and if she wasn't a local, she shouldn't be wandering around on her own. It was easy to get lost. Even being born here, Hazeleigh had always been cautioned not to go too far alone as a girl.

She followed. The girl kept walking deeper into Peterson land. Hazeleigh hesitated, but… This girl could hardly be *luring* her into something bad. If she was, she was in something bad herself and maybe Hazeleigh could help.

So she kept following.

Eventually the girl stopped, as if she knew just where she was going. She scrambled up a little pile of rocks and then disappeared behind them. Hazeleigh was mired in indecision. None of this felt particularly right, but she couldn't bring herself to leave the girl alone.

When the girl climbed back over the rocks, she had two things in her hands. Hazeleigh didn't remember packing her pink mittens in her backpack, but they were hers. Likely they'd been put in the pack sometime back in the middle of winter and Hazeleigh had just forgotten to take them out.

The flashlight had probably been in Landon's bag, as it wasn't Hazeleigh's and it looked suitably heavy and military-grade. Something Landon would definitely have.

The girl held them out. Her gaze was on the items, like she was loathe to give them up. But she knew it was the right thing to do and she was doing it.

Hazeleigh knew she could use both items. A flashlight and mittens. They would definitely come in handy, but the girl…

Hazeleigh waved a hand. "Keep them."

The girl looked at Hazeleigh in confusion. "Why?"

"If you took them, you must really need them. Besides, I have more."

The girl chewed on her bottom lip. "But…they're yours."

"Do you need them?"

The girl nodded slowly. "It'd help my mom to have them."

"So take them. I'll be okay without them." Hazeleigh offered a reassuring smile.

"Okay, well, thanks." The girl hesitated. "I have to get back to my mom."

Hazeleigh had to stop herself from reaching forward, out to the girl. "Do you know how to get there?"

The girl nodded. She even began to walk away, then she stopped and turned. "Please don't follow me. I know where I'm going."

Since following was exactly what she'd been planning to do, Hazeleigh was surprised the little girl was astute enough to realize that. "It's easy to get lost out here."

"I know. They won't let me get lost."

Hazeleigh thought it should be comforting, but there was something sad about the way the girl said *let*. "What's your name?"

The girl shook her head. And then she ran.

LANDON WAS BEYOND irritated it took him hours to return to Hazeleigh. But he'd needed to eat, to get more computer elements together, then collect things on the down low. Dry clothes that would fit Hazeleigh, more food and water, a blanket, a heavy jacket. Plus a few things for Buttercup, so Hazeleigh could have her out there for the next few days.

The sun was already setting when he finally got to

his horse. Everyone else was inside, eating dinner, trying to talk Zara out of going down to the police station to yell at…well, everyone.

Landon was still amazed by Zara's loyalty. He knew that Zara's personality was just…like a bulldozer, but it was more than that. She loved her sister wholly and unconditionally and was going to stand up for her no matter what.

Landon had found that in his military brothers later in life, with other men who'd had no unconditional familial love to speak of, so it still baffled him when it came from blood. Particularly when he knew, from town gossip, that Hazeleigh and Zara's father had left them high and dry when it came to selling the ranch.

Maybe it was the triplet thing, particularly since Amberleigh had been murdered. Hazeleigh and Zara had to stick together extra now. Their love for one another was born of experience as much as genetics.

Not that anything he'd dealt with as a child had brought him closer to his biological brothers. The family he'd been born into wanted to make anyone else hurt the way they did, and though Landon had dealt with some dark times, he'd never had that mean streak.

He rode his horse a little faster than necessary, trying to leave the past and thoughts about love and protection far behind him.

He had a mystery to solve.

When he arrived at the schoolhouse, Buttercup was nowhere to be seen. His instincts began to hum. Something was wrong.

He could deal with wrong, though. He was a soldier. He would handle whatever this was. The important thing was to focus. He got off his horse and searched the schoolhouse, but didn't find any sign of Hazeleigh. Even the bags were gone.

Had she...taken off on him?

Shock and anger and fear all mixed together, because he didn't know what conclusion to jump to. Had the person who'd shot at them taken her? Had something spooked her, and she'd run? Or had she just... run, like she'd been planning to do in the beginning?

He swung back on his horse. She wouldn't, which meant someone was after her.

He looked around the grass for prints. He took his horse over to where Buttercup had been tied and saw the telltale sign of horse tracks, moving away from the schoolhouse.

It hadn't been at a run. Landon tried to let that deduction settle him. He followed. It only took a short trot to see what made his blood run cold.

Buttercup, tied to another tree not far away. The bags next to some rocks. No sign of Hazeleigh *anywhere*.

Focus. Calm. He repeated the words over and over, trying to will his military training to take over, but a cold, overwhelming fear had gotten into his bones. He swung off the horse, tied him to where Buttercup was tethered and touched the horse.

"What went on here?"

Of course, the horse didn't answer or seem perturbed at all. This should have calmed Landon, but it didn't. He found some tracks in the grass—hard to pick up, but enough of a depression to see two sets of prints. But one was so...small. It didn't make any sense. The less sense it made, the more panic took over.

He followed the tracks, trying to will his heartbeat to slow enough so he could hear. Listen. Figure this out. But his breathing came in little pants as a million terrible bloody scenarios worked through his mind.

He kept walking, kept panicking, and by the time he saw a flash of pink scarf, like yesterday, when he'd seen her running, all rational thought fled his mind.

She was running. If he could think straight, he'd realize it was not the same breakneck speed, but something more like a jog. But he'd lost hold of rationality a while back.

He scanned the area, looking for a threat, his hand on the gun he'd holstered under his shirt. He pulled it out, ready for anything.

She finally looked up. "Landon." She stopped on a dime, like she thought he was going to shoot her. Like she was *surprised* to see him.

He wanted to shake her. He wanted to hold her to him until his heart stopped skipping every other beat in utter terror.

"Get behind me," he ordered.

She blinked and rushed behind him. "What are you looking for?" she asked in a whisper.

"What am I…?" He looked over his shoulder at her. "What happened? Where did you go?"

"I…" She looked at the gun, then at him. "You could probably put that away if this is just about me."

He turned slowly, holstering the gun with more care than was necessary as it began to dawn on him. "You weren't running from anything?"

"No, I was running back. I didn't want you to worry, so I was trying to hurry and—"

"What the hell were you thinking?" he demanded, and he couldn't keep his hands off her shoulders. He didn't shake her, though he wanted to. He just…had to make sure she was really here and whole and *fine*.

Then, as if she'd heard his thoughts, she reiterated them. She patted his chest gently while he gripped her shoulders. "I'm fine, Landon. It's all right."

And she was. Perfectly fine. Standing here, not bloody and not dead, not even pale or scared. Just here and trying not to worry him and… The dam just broke—all the things he'd kept such a tight lid on since the first time she'd smiled at him, and it had felt like a damn *thunder strike*.

He kissed her. Because it felt right and solid and reassuring.

Fine. All right. That's what she'd said.

None of this was any of those things.

But her mouth was. The way she melted against him was just right. She tasted like the promise of spring and felt like salvation, and everything disappeared except the feel of her mouth under his. Like everything might be okay from this moment on.

But nothing was okay because they were in the middle of nowhere, hiding from her family and the police, with the threat of someone who wanted her to take the fall for a murder.

He pulled back, shocked to his core that he'd gotten so…out of control. Not just the kiss, but the last twenty minutes he'd…come unglued. That was unacceptable. "I am…so sorry."

"You're…sorry," she repeated, her tone devoid of

emotion. Or maybe he was so lost in his own lack of control he couldn't think about anyone else's emotions.

"I… You weren't there and I…" He raked his fingers through his hair, trying to find a center he was usually so good at finding. "I panicked. It's no excuse, but I was just…" He didn't know. He was at a complete and utter loss. Everything from the point of her not being at the schoolhouse to here was *madness*. And his fault. His utterly idiotic, uncontrolled fault.

"Does your cure for panic often involve kissing women?"

He blew out a breath. Her amusement mixed with a kind of haughty cool disdain brought him down. She was fine. He was being irrational, sure, but she was fine. And just a little irritated with him—and he didn't think it was about the kiss so much as his reaction to it.

"No." He paused and took a bolstering breath before he said, "You know, I'm usually charming and smooth. But with you… Why the hell do I fumble?"

Her mouth curved. "I don't know, but it's kind of cute."

"Cute?" He groaned. "Put me out of my misery while I've still got time."

She laughed, and he thought maybe they could find some even, sane ground *somewhere*.

"You don't have to apologize for kissing me. I didn't exactly push you away."

"You didn't."

She stared up at him and this time *she* was the one who fumbled. She stepped back a little bit, broke eye contact. "There was a girl," she blurted. "A little girl. Maybe ten years old? She'd gone through our bags, stolen a few things."

"I'm sorry, I don't follow. What?"

She explained. A little girl. Stolen items. Wanting to help, but the girl telling her not to. "Then she just took off on me. I… Something wasn't right there." Hazeleigh looked back to where she'd been coming from. "I feel like I should *do* something. She wasn't old enough to be tramping around by herself."

"You'd be surprised what kids are capable of."

She looked back at him, her gaze drifting down to his chest. Though it was covered by his coat and sweatshirt, he knew she was thinking about his scar.

Something he wasn't ready to talk about right now. Bad enough he'd told her this morning. Now with that kiss ricocheting through him, he just…

They needed to move beyond the kiss. Maybe she'd kissed him back, but she'd also put distance between them. Because the moment wasn't right. They had a lot of things to figure out before anything about that could be…made right.

"It'll work in our favor," he said instead, keeping himself stiff. "I go back to the ranch in the morning, say I had your encounter with the little girl and I spent the evening trying to find her. Then one of my brothers can look into it and find her, make sure everything's okay."

"If they find her and she says she spoke to a woman who claimed to be Zara Hart, they'll know it was me out here. They'll know you're with me."

"You pretended to be Zara?" He didn't know why that pleased him, only that he would have liked to have seen it. Hazeleigh purposefully engaging in some subterfuge would be entertaining.

"I didn't know what else to do. And Amberleigh and

I used to practice being each other all the time. Triplets prerogative."

"But not Zara?"

Hazeleigh huffed out a laugh. "She always refused to dress like us, and said she was quite happy being herself. But we'd pretend to be her, each other, to see what we could get away with."

"Are you telling me underneath all that good-girl exterior there's a secret bad girl lurking?"

She laughed. "Not exactly, but Amberleigh could bring it out in me." Her smile was warm and fond and sad, and he wanted to hold her again, so he cleared his throat and shoved his hands into his pockets.

"Let's get back to the schoolhouse before dark. I've got some things for us to go over on my computer." He resisted the urge to slide his arm around her shoulders or reach for her hand. Best to keep all those physical responses to a necessary basis and this was definitely not necessary.

No matter how much he wanted it to be.

"What kind of things?" she asked, falling into step next to him but keeping a good distance between their bodies as they walked back to Buttercup.

"I'm going to hack into the police server and try to get photos of the crime scene. I've been working on tracing the call that implicated you. We'll see what they've got."

"Photos of the crime scene would include…"

"You don't have to look at Mr. Field, Hazeleigh. We can figure this out without you going through that again."

"But do you think it would help if I did?"

Landon sighed. He could lie, but… "I don't really know. You might see something no one else would notice, but there might not be anything there. I can describe what I see to you and—"

"I can do it." She nodded, as if convincing herself. "I can do it. If it gives us answers, I can look at it. Mr. Field deserves answers, and so do I."

Chapter Twelve

Landon didn't say anything to her after that. They walked in silence back to Buttercup, then they walked with her to the schoolhouse. Settled the horses, fed and watered them with the supplies Landon had brought.

He insisted she change her clothes even though hers had mostly dried out. He'd brought her one of his own sweatshirts and a pair of Zara's jeans he'd snagged from the wash. Her underwear and bra were still a damp clump in the bag. The bra was no problem, but she was hardly going to put on jeans without underwear. So she switched out her shirt for Landon's, but kept her skirt on and tried to find a somewhat secluded area to smooth out her underthings so they'd eventually dry.

Once she let Landon in, he turned on a battery-powered camping lantern. He pulled a blanket out of the duffel he'd brought and settled it on her lap.

Hazeleigh found herself speechless at the small, sweet act.

He said nothing and went through setting up his computer equipment. All sorts of things she didn't understand—especially considering there was no power source out here. But *he* clearly knew what he was doing.

"How do you…know how to do all of this?"

He looked up briefly, but he was distracted, clearly uninterested in her presence at the moment. That shouldn't have bothered her. So he'd kissed her like she was oxygen? Clearly, he could turn passion on and off and that was *fine*.

She scowled.

He turned his gaze back to his machines, shrugging. "Training."

"What kind of training?" she persisted.

"Computer training."

That was *not* an answer. In fact, it was a very purposeful *non*answer, but he was so focused it seemed pointless to push him on it. They had more important things to focus on.

Crime scene photos.

She swallowed at her queasy stomach. She didn't want to relive it, at all, but if she saw something no one else would notice, how could she avoid it?

She had to be brave and do what she could, because Mr. Field was dead. As much as her brain couldn't let go of her worry over the little girl, Landon was right. Kids could take care of themselves when they had the tools, and that girl had seemed to have all the tools she needed.

As for the kiss… She glanced at Landon out of her peripheral vision. He had a serious expression as he studied the computer screen.

She'd never been kissed like that. With urgency, but…gently. There had been desire, but it hadn't been *about* sex.

He'd kissed her as if it had soothed something inside

of him. He had *kissed her*, and she had backed off when he looked like he might do it again. An inner-flight response she wasn't particularly thrilled with right now because it had been a *great* kiss. All-encompassing and real, and she hadn't thought about her nerves.

She'd simply enjoyed. Her brain kept insisting something had to be wrong with it—him, her, it. But her heart was telling her other things. She had no idea which one to trust.

"It occurred to me last night there might be something to go on if we can see what Mr. Field was researching and connect it to the missing files," Landon said, fiddling with wires and tapping at his keyboard. "He was murdered at work, when it would have been easier and more isolated to murder him at home. I'm still working on the phone call, but it's a lot of dead ends. Whoever made that call made sure to hide themselves."

Hazeleigh's stomach churned. She'd been here before. Framed for something she didn't do. She didn't understand it—she was hardly *murderer* material— but it was clear someone wanted her to take the fall.

And the thing that connected her and Mr. Field was his research. Very little else.

"But we know something about Mr. Field caused him to be a target. This was not a random homicide. Or the person who shot at us wouldn't have gone to his house."

Hazeleigh sucked in a breath. She didn't want to see Mr. Field there again. It was vivid enough in her memories, but if it would help, if it would offer a clue… "I can do it."

He looked up at her, his blue eyes direct and compassionate. "I know you can. Doesn't mean you have to. I blocked out the body. You'll still see some of the blood, but you won't have to see him. Okay?"

"Okay, but... I have to do whatever I can to figure out who did this to him. I *have* to."

He gave her shoulder a quick squeeze. "Okay." He turned the screen toward her. He had blocked out Mr. Field's body, but she could still see it in her mind. She could still smell it. Feel the shock and terror and grief welling up inside of her.

Until a steady pressure broke through the fog of panic. "Breathe, Hazeleigh," Landon instructed, his hand still on her shoulder. Always offering that anchor she needed.

She wished she could be strong enough to be her own anchor, but she thought about Zara. Stronger than anyone Hazeleigh knew. So certain, so determined. She fought for anything and everything.

And she'd learned to lean on Jake. She *loved* Jake. In a way, it had made Zara stronger. Because she didn't have to take everything on her own shoulders. Maybe leaning had some strength in it, if Hazeleigh ever learned to lean on the right people.

She sucked in a breath, let it out slowly when Landon told her to. She knew he was about to tell her she didn't have to do this, again, so she really focused on that breathing. On the facts, not her feelings.

"What am I looking for?"

"What was he looking at? It looks like some kind of photo album," Landon said, pointing to the desk. Most of it was blacked out to hide Mr. Field's head, which was slumped over the pages.

"Yes, it's the album that's usually kept in that box I told you about." She pointed to it in the frame of the picture. It was open and splattered with blood in the background. "It would have been in there. So Mr. Field must have been studying the photographs when he was shot."

She didn't want to say the rest, but knew she had to. She looked back at Landon, meeting his steady blue gaze. "You need to let me see the whole picture."

"Haze—"

She shook her head and cut off his objection. "I already saw it. I can't erase it. If I can help, I need to see. Your blackout blocks are hiding most of the album. I know his head is hiding some of it, too." Hazeleigh swallowed. "But if I can make out the pictures and the page he's on, maybe we have a clue."

Landon looked pained, but he nodded and then clicked a few keys on his keyboard. Mr. Field's slumped form, bloody and dead, appeared.

Hazeleigh swallowed down her body's revolt. The photo album might be a clue. She studied the pictures, trying to pretend Mr. Field wasn't in the photo. "This is the page with pictures of…" She trailed off. Was it just a coincidence?

"What?"

"It's the album of places they thought the gold might be. This page is photos of Peterson land." She cleared her dry throat. "Where this schoolhouse is. Where the girl was." Surely a little girl didn't connect to Mr. Field's murder.

"Why?" Landon asked. "Why would he be looking at pictures of Peterson land in his photo album?"

"One of the theories is the robber was a local, someone everyone knew, who just hid the gold on his land. Johannes Peterson was one of the suspects. These are pictures of his house, and... One's missing."

"One what? Picture?"

Hazeleigh nodded, squinting as she leaned closer to the screen. She couldn't make out the page number on the album, due to blood and poor Mr. Field's hair, but she'd organized that album. She could figure it out. She pointed at the space where a picture should have been. "Right here. The murderer must have taken it."

"Mr. Field wouldn't have taken the pictures out himself to look at?"

"No. They were delicate enough as it was. That album is archival grade, and it protects the historical artifacts from further damage," she explained to Landon. "He wouldn't have removed the photo without gloves." Or without a threat leveled at him.

"So whoever killed him took that one picture," Landon said. "Do you know what it was of?"

"I can figure it out." The grain of this picture was too fuzzy, and she couldn't read the page numbers, but it wasn't impossible. "Probably."

"Did Mr. Field have digital copies of these pictures? The album?"

"He didn't," Hazeleigh said, and there was hope struggling to sprout for the first time in days. "But I did." She pushed out a shaky breath. "The thing is, Mr. Field had found them...somewhat illegally in the attic before they condemned the Peterson house. No one would know he had those aside from me."

As it was the first lead they'd had, they both jumped into action. Landon didn't have time to think about anything else. Hazeleigh had copies on her work laptop, which she'd left back in her cabin. Easy enough for him to grab, especially at night.

She was confident—or at least tried to act confident—that she could figure out the missing picture. Something about Peterson land. Which was where they were.

Landon didn't believe in coincidences when it came to murder and framing innocent people. It all had to connect.

But right now he had a lot of pieces he *knew* connected, but didn't have a clue as to *how*.

"It has to be a Peterson, doesn't it?" Landon went through the rest of the pictures he'd hacked, to make sure the photo album wasn't clearer on any of them. Then he went through the list of the items the police had collected from the office.

"Johannes had twelve sons. Only three of them stayed here in Wyoming. Two died young and without children, although there was always a rumor that Lars was *really* the father of Mrs. Minnie Harper's youngest. If I ignore that rumor, Oscar had six kids." She continued naming people, as if he had any idea who she was talking about.

"I'm sorry. You lost me somewhere around Oscar."

She smiled indulgently. "Yeah, I get that a lot. The bottom line is there aren't any Petersons in Wilde anymore. So if it does connect to the Petersons and that long-ago theory, it's not someone local." She frowned, clearly thinking about something else as she said it.

"What?"

"It just seems to me… Whoever this person is, if it has to do with those pictures and the bank robbery, knew an awful lot. I suppose it could have been someone Mr. Field was communicating with online, but he usually had me do his typing for him, and he hasn't had anyone interested in the Peterson theory communicate with him in years. Far more people are interested in the prostitute theory."

"There's a prostitute theory?"

She rolled her eyes. "Why does everyone always get excited about the prostitute theory?"

"Well, it's all very *Tombstone*, isn't it? Bank robberies and ladies of the night and dashing cowboys." He tipped his own hat, making her laugh as he'd hoped.

He knew she was sad about Mr. Field, hurt and worried about everything going on. If he could get her to laugh every once in a while, it would do them both some good.

"I suppose it is."

"Is it possible Mr. Field had emails or communication he didn't tell you about?"

Hazeleigh frowned. "Well, I suppose anything's possible. I suppose he had to have, because I'm the only one I know of who knew he had these." She chewed on her lip for a moment, distracting him into thinking about when he'd kissed her earlier.

He blinked and looked back down at his computer screen.

Get up to 4
FREE FABULOUS BOOKS
You Love!

To thank you for being a loyal reader we'd like to send you up to 4 FREE BOOKS, absolutely free when you try the Harlequin Reader Service.

Just write "YES" on the Loyal Reader Voucher and we'll send you 2 free books from each series you choose and Free Mystery Gifts, altogether worth over $20.

Try **Harlequin® Romantic Suspense** books featuring heart-racing page-turners with unexpected plot twists and irresistible chemistry that will keep you guessing to the very end.

Try **Harlequin Intrigue® Larger-Print** books featuring action-packed stories that will keep you on the edge of your seat. Solve the crime and deliver justice at all costs.

Or **TRY BOTH and get 2 books from each series!**

Your free books are completely free, even the shipping! If you continue with your subscription, you can look forward to curated monthly shipments of brand-new books from your selected series, always at a discount off the cover price! Plus you can cancel any time.

So don't miss out, return your Loyal Readers Voucher today to get your Free books.

Pam Powers

LOYAL READER
FREE BOOKS VOUCHER

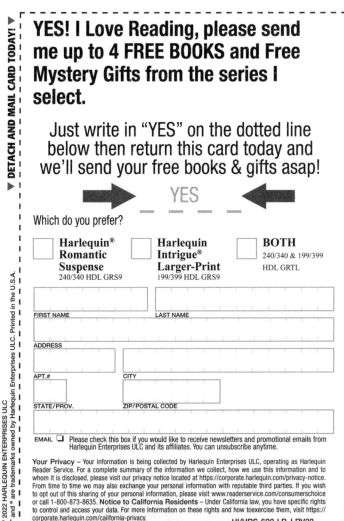

HARLEQUIN® Reader Service —Here's how it works:

Accepting your 2 free books and 2 free gifts (gifts valued at approximately $10.00 retail) places you under no obligation to buy anything. You may keep the books and gifts and return the shipping statement marked "cancel." If you do not cancel, approximately one month later we'll send you more books from the series you have chosen, and bill you at our low, subscribers-only discount price. Harlequin® Romantic Suspense books consist of 4 books each month and cost just $5.49 each in the U.S. or $6.24 each in Canada, a savings of at least 12% off the cover price. Harlequin Intrigue® Larger-Print books consist of 6 books each month and cost just $6.49 each in the U.S. or $6.99 each in Canada, a savings of at least 13% off the cover price. It's quite a bargain! Shipping and handling is just 50¢ per book in the U.S. and $1.25 per book in Canada*. You may return any shipment at our expense and cancel at any time by calling the number below — or you may continue to receive monthly shipments at our low, subscribers-only discount price plus shipping and handling.

▲ If offer card is missing write to: Harlequin Reader Service, P.O. Box 1341, Buffalo, NY 14240-8531 or visit www.ReaderService.com ▲

BUSINESS REPLY MAIL
FIRST-CLASS MAIL   PERMIT NO. 717   BUFFALO, NY

POSTAGE WILL BE PAID BY ADDRESSEE

HARLEQUIN READER SERVICE
PO BOX 1341
BUFFALO NY 14240-8571

NO POSTAGE
NECESSARY
IF MAILED
IN THE
UNITED STATES

"The thing is, I have access to his emails. So if he had a secret, I doubt it would have been hidden there."

"Maybe I can check phone records." He added that to his mental list of things to research. "When I get you your computer, could you access his emails?"

"If I had an internet connection."

Landon nodded. Thanks to his *training,* he could handle that. Even out here with no electricity and service. The beauty of military-grade technology. "I'll go. Get your computer. It might be a while since I might have to stop into the ranch to keep anyone from getting suspicious. I want you to get some rest. I'll set up a lock and alarm on the door, so you'll be safe."

She didn't agree, just stared at him for a long while, expression grave. When she spoke, her voice was firm. "I want to go with you to get my computer."

He shook his head. "It's an unnecessary risk and you have to be exhausted."

"If I'm exhausted, you're just as exhausted."

He opened his mouth, *this close* to making a quip about military training and lack of sleep, but she wasn't supposed to *know* that. He needed to get a handle on wanting to tell her things.

"It's a half-hour ride," she said, and clearly she'd been thinking this through. "That gives us plenty of nightfall to make sure we don't get caught. I know just where the laptop is without you fumbling around my cabin or leaving prints. It's just like the fort. Best to take me."

He didn't agree with her in this case, but he also suspected her insistence on going had something to do with looking at Mr. Field's murdered body for far longer than he'd wanted her to and being left here in the dark alone.

"I'm not worried about the cops. We can handle avoiding them. I can't promise you we can get through your cabin without one of my brothers getting wise and stopping us."

"So you'll go into the ranch house and make sure they don't."

"Hazeleigh."

"I can get through my cabin and grab the computer in ten minutes flat. It will take you much longer, at least twenty minutes, which gives your brothers far more time to *get wise*."

"It would hardly take me twenty," he muttered irritably. Mostly because she wasn't wrong. But that didn't make *him* wrong. "You're the one on the run. And I know you want to keep Zara out of this. I can convince her I'm working on my own if you're not there. If she sees you? All bets are off."

Hazeleigh shook her head, unmoved. "I won't sleep. I won't rest. I'll worry. I'll obsess. I need to be a part of this. When I was accused of murder last year, I sat in a holding cell and just answered all these questions. While Zara and Jake, and then you and your brothers, all risked your lives for *me*. I can't do that again."

"I'm not risking my life."

She stepped forward and put her hand on his arm—where his bandage was underneath the sleeve. "Someone shot you. This is *all* a risk."

Her brown eyes held his. And she was just… He didn't have the words.

He wanted to protect her, but it was bigger than that.

He wanted to find her a life where she wouldn't need protecting. Where maybe it could just be them. He could make her laugh and she could worry over him and they could…just be.

All his years in the military, all the pain and loss and stress of coming to Wyoming and building a new life had made the simple act of *being* his biggest goal. She made it sweeter.

And now was not the time. But she moved closer, her one hand staying on his arm, and the other one coming up to his chest. And she didn't look down, like she was remembering the scar underneath. She held his gaze instead.

And angled her mouth to his…

Chapter Thirteen

Hazeleigh didn't know what she was doing. There were far more important things going on, and besides, she was probably reading things all wrong. Somehow.

But she wanted…that feeling from before. All-encompassing heat and a giddy kind of settling. Like *finally* something would be okay. She knew it wouldn't be, but she wanted to chase the feeling anyway.

This isn't the answer, that nasty little voice in her head said. *It's a distraction. For him. For you. There's nothing here.*

Usually when her brain and heart were at odds, she didn't have the faintest clue what to listen to, but there was something else here today. Zara would probably call it her *gut*, and it wanted to kiss him, just as much as her always too-soft heart wanted her to as well.

So she did. She rose to her tiptoes and pressed her mouth to his, still holding on to his arm. His hands came up to frame her face, angling her just so as he kissed her. It wasn't *just* like outside when he'd found her. This was calmer, more gentle.

And yet the kiss spread through her like a warm fire on a cold night. Something inside of her clicked. A lock being opened. Or closed maybe. She didn't know, only that something inside of her eased. Settled. *Yes*.

She clutched him as he led her to everywhere she wanted to go in the short space of a kiss. And there was nothing but this, him. She could forget it all, just exist in this space where their mouths touched.

For eternity. For far too short a time.

Landon eased away, but held her still, his fingers all tangled in her hair, his eyes only half-open. "You don't know how long I've wanted to do that," he murmured, still just a whisper from her mouth.

"Long?" His hands were still in her hair and her heart was still pounding so hard she wasn't sure she'd made out the words correctly. He kissed her cheek, her jaw. She wanted to melt into the floor, but... "You've wanted to kiss me for...a long time?"

"Ages," he said, his mouth pressing against her neck and making her shiver. He held her like she was precious, and there was no nasty sharp possessiveness to it. It was just sweetness. She knew he had edges—she'd seen them. But when it came to her...

You're fooling yourself again, Hazeleigh.

But it wasn't *hard* to fool herself. She used to have to really work at it to convince herself a man cared. She didn't have to try at all to believe Landon did. She was trying to convince herself that he didn't.

And isn't that far more dangerous?

But she couldn't quite believe the voice in her head. Not when he was saying he'd wanted to kiss her for *ages*. "Since when?"

He didn't release her, but he did stop kissing her.

He looked down at her. "Well. When we first got here, you were so skittish."

She frowned, hating that the descriptor was correct. *Skittish*. Landon had arrived right after she'd broken up with Douglas, and she *had* been skittish. As she tried to figure out why she always picked the wrong guy, what kind of danger she might be in, she'd wanted a lot of distance from *all* men.

"And I'd try to get a smile out of you. Make a joke. Show off. Whatever I thought might get a smile, but you never did. You were always so serious. Then I was in the stables singing some dumb song to the horses and I looked over and there you were. Just smiling at me."

She remembered. It had been a few months ago. Kate had settled into the ranch and Hazeleigh had started to believe something…nice might have happened out of the Thompsons moving onto the ranch. Zara and Jake. Kate and Brody.

But she'd felt lonely, and a little outnumbered by all the *men* around. She'd come out to the stables to give Buttercup a treat, a rare occurrence since the Thompson brothers' arrival. It had taken screwing up some courage, and believing the Thompsons were elsewhere.

Most of them had been on that occasion. Except Landon. He'd been in the stables, singing to the horses. A song she hadn't recognized, and half suspected he'd made up himself. She'd watched him for a moment or two, perfectly in tune with the horses while he crooned to them.

It had warmed her to him considerably—the singing, the way the horses reacted to him. The moment had broken down some of her defenses. Or maybe she'd

just finally been ready to *let* them down and his way
with the horses reminded her that she could.

"You have a nice voice."

His mouth quirked up. "That's what you said then.
With a smile. And it just…hit me. Harder than it should
have. I don't know what that was. I've tried to figure it
out, but it's… I don't have the words for it. Only that it
made me crave your smiles. It made me want…to find
a way to be around you without making you nervous."

It was hard to believe Landon had been standing
around…craving *anything* from her. But she'd been
wrapped up in her own stuff, and if she looked back,
well… He had always gone out of his way to make
her smile.

But she was still *her* and that was still a bit of a
mess. She felt the driving need to be up front about
that. "I have…"

He raised an eyebrow. Like he remembered her
blurting out yesterday she had terrible taste in men.

It didn't feel fair right now because he wasn't terrible taste at all. But she was still…her. "I have issues,"
she admitted lamely.

He chuckled, but it wasn't his normal, happy chuckle.
"Don't we all?"

She could leave it at that. She could do a lot of things
in this moment, but she swallowed and told him a truth
she hadn't even told her sister. "I don't really know how
to trust myself."

He studied her, as if that wasn't a terrible thing to be.
So unsure, so lacking confidence and strength of purpose.

But he still didn't let her go. "You said you trusted me."

She nodded. "I do."

"We can start there." He sighed, like he gravely regretted what he had to say next. "But for tonight, we've got about six hours of dark, and we'll need them all to get your laptop."

LANDON ALMOST LAUGHED at the way her mouth turned into something very close to a pout. Laughed because he wanted to pout a bit himself. Or maybe punch a few holes in the wall. He wanted to say screw the laptop and murder cases and spend the rest of the night learning each other.

But it wasn't an answer, and he didn't want to be...a distraction. Something she could excuse away later. If he had a chance with Hazeleigh, he wanted a real one.

Which meant proving, once and for all, that she was no killer. And hopefully, somewhere in all that, she could learn to trust herself the way she so clearly wanted to.

"You said we. I hope that means you agree with me about me going with."

He wanted to scowl, but he managed to keep his mouth impassive. With a mountain of regret, he pulled his hands away from her face and took a step back. "It's not that I don't think you're right about being quicker—"

"Excellent. It's settled, then." She strode for the door like she could steamroll him into bringing her. And there was something about her trying to steamroll him that made him want to let her.

It was dangerous, but so was leaving her here...even if he set up an alarm for her. And maybe if she could do this, be involved, she could trust herself.

Or maybe he'd lost all his good sense and was putting her in danger just because he wanted to be with her. And that was the kind of split focus Cal had forever been warning them about back in their military days.

This *was* like those days. It was about finding the truth, protecting the innocent. It required focus and strength of purpose and not letting anything compromise clearheaded decisions.

But that kiss still lingered, and the way she'd held onto him, sighed against him. Been wide-eyed asking him how long he'd wanted to kiss her, as if she couldn't imagine such a thing. And he wasn't in the military any longer. People had shot at them, a man was dead, but it still wasn't the same.

He was a person. Not a soldier.

He wasn't sure he knew what to do with that, but Hazeleigh was already outside the schoolhouse, getting Buttercup ready in the silvery moonlight.

He walked to his horse, hating the uncertainty that swirled within him. "Hazeleigh…"

"I'm doing this," she said simply. "I don't need your permission any more than you needed my permission to help me against my will."

He supposed she had a point there. "Can you at least do it my way?"

"And what is your way?" she asked, primly enough to make him smile.

"We'll ride the horses to the stables. You give me time to do a perimeter check, see where everyone is, and then we devise a plan from there. *Maybe* it's you going into your cabin and getting your laptop, but maybe it's something else." He couldn't make out her expression in the dark, so he simply had to wait for her response.

"Perimeter check," she echoed.

"Yes, it's when I—"

"I think I can figure out what a perimeter check is. What I can't figure out is why you talk like that, talk like you know how to handle *murderers* and gunshot wounds, and have all that fancy computer equipment I've never seen outside a movie."

Landon didn't have the faintest idea how to respond. The truth wanted to tumble out. He wanted to lay it all at her feet.

But that wasn't allowed.

You're a person now, not a soldier.

But he was still a member of Team Breaker. Whether they were a team or a family, he'd made an oath.

Do you think Jake and Brody have kept that oath?

"Landon?"

He swallowed at all this *feeling*—which was bad to have. He had so much to accomplish without emotion getting in the way.

"I just need you to agree to follow instructions."

It was her turn to be quiet for a shade too long. "I'll be honest—I'm a little tired of following everyone else's instructions."

"I'm only trying to keep you safe."

"Especially when they're meant to keep me safe. Does it occur to anyone I might want to stay safe myself? Kind of why I ran away."

"And does it occur to you that people want to keep you safe because they care?" He managed to keep his voice as even as possible, though all this conflicting sentiment was still coursing through him.

She inhaled sharply, and there was a poignant silence where he thought she might ask just what he meant by *care*. But she didn't.

She let out the breath. "Yes, I know. All right. I promise to follow instructions with one caveat. You won't take any unnecessary risks for me."

"Define unnecessary."

She sighed heavily. "You always have a comeback."

"That I do. Now, time is wasting. Let's get going." He made sure she was on Buttercup before he mounted his own horse. They both knew the way back to the ranch and Hazeleigh's cabin, so she didn't lead him or vice versa. They kept their horses abreast of each other and began an easy trot in the direction of the cabin.

"Landon, I keep thinking about…"

Landon braced himself for a mention of the kiss, a conversation about what it all meant, but apparently *she'd* forgotten all about it.

"The little girl."

Landon shifted, trying to ignore the disappointment coursing through him. He should be *relieved* she wanted to talk about mysteries, not kisses and feelings. "I know you're worried that she's on her own, but if she seemed okay…"

"No, it isn't that. Or it isn't only that she was alone. It's just… That first day I went into the schoolhouse I thought it looked off. It wasn't as dusty as it should have been. Like someone had been in there, sweeping up."

"You think it was her?"

"I don't know what to think. But if Mr. Field's murder really does connect with this silly old bank robbery, and that bank robbery really did connect to the Petersons back in the day, isn't it odd that there are people hiding and sneaking about on Peterson land?"

"People or a child?"

"She mentioned her mother. That the flashlight and mittens would help her mother."

"Well, then, she isn't alone."

"I suppose not." Landon didn't have to see her to know she was frowning. She remained quiet for the next few moments, but he knew she hadn't stopped thinking about the girl.

"I guess the important question is, regardless of the girl, why are people hiding on Peterson land? *Any* people."

Landon had wondered that himself, but he didn't know enough of the town or family dynamics to determine if that was strange or not. "Did Mr. Field have any connection to any Petersons? Any emails he might have sent about the theory?"

"Not to my knowledge. And I'm not saying Mr. Field told me everything, but I did organize his life. It seems… unlikely there was something going on I didn't know about."

Landon considered that. He wished he could believe it. But there had to be *something* Hazeleigh didn't know or she'd have some theories about why someone might kill Mr. Field.

"It wouldn't be out of the realm of possibility that it's a bit of a random thing. There are those treasure-hunter-type people, always on the lookout for old gold or what have you. Sometimes obsessed people get desperate and sometimes desperate people murder."

Hazeleigh considered it. "A desperate treasure hunter would be…desperate, right? It would be about the obsession or frustration, but we know this had to be a little premeditated or how would they know to frame me for it?"

Landon wished he knew.

Chapter Fourteen

They didn't speak much after that. Every question Hazeleigh had just took them in circles and she was tired of the circles. She was tired of not knowing what to fight against.

She knew part of why she was tired was because Landon had kissed her. Suddenly she had something... to look forward to. She didn't want to run. She wanted this to be over so she could...figure out what life might look like with Landon in it.

A *good* man. Who liked *her*.

She rolled her eyes at herself. Timing was everything, and hers continued to be terrible. What did she even have after this? Mr. Field was dead, which meant she was *jobless*, and... He was gone.

The waves of grief came at odd points, washing over her. It still didn't feel real.

But they rode through a beautiful starry Wyoming night and Hazeleigh had some...hope maybe, that they could figure out this mystery. The album was a clue. Maybe if she got into Mr. Field's emails, they'd find another. Maybe, just maybe, she could help solve this and feel like she'd done something for Mr. Field, since she couldn't go back in time and save him.

Since her bad feeling hadn't saved him.

She resolutely pushed away the thoughts that wanted to follow, most in her father's voice about what good she was if she couldn't use that bad feeling to help the people she loved.

She couldn't go back in time. So she could only move forward. She stroked Buttercup's mane and allowed herself to relax into the saddle. She was exhausted. Wrung out and a little jumpy, but there was this driving need inside of her to keep going.

She needed an answer. *Some* kind of explanation.

The ranch came into view in the moonlight. Just shadows, but the shadows of her childhood and adolescence. Amberleigh had loved to sneak out of the house at this time of night and sometimes Hazeleigh had been brave enough to go with her—never off the ranch, like Amberleigh often did, but to sneak around the stables or their grandparents' cabin, giggling and feeling like cat burglars.

Hazeleigh sighed at the pain in her chest. Amberleigh hadn't been perfect, but she'd been…vivacious. Hazeleigh had always felt alive around her. She'd been brave with Amberleigh.

Now Amberleigh was dead and Hazeleigh was here. Still right here. For years she'd been hiding away in plain sight, and it suddenly struck her as very, very wrong.

"We'll stop here," Landon said while they were still a little way from the cabin. But they were behind the stables, which would hide them from just about any view from the house.

"You stay right here while I put the horses up. They'll water, feed, rest. If someone comes, you stay right here, hidden as best you can."

"Why would anyone come out here in the middle of the night?"

Landon was quiet for a moment, and she heard his quiet footfalls as he got off his horse. She waited for him to come to her. He took her hand and helped her off the horse. She didn't need the help to get off so much as she did for the landing, since she couldn't see the ground beneath her—the stable blocked most of the bright moonlight.

He held her steady when she stepped a little wrong and stumbled. Part of her wanted to lean into him. Give up. Go inside. Let everyone in that house take care of everything while she slept.

But she was done being a coward. So she found her own two feet, gave his arm a grateful squeeze and then stepped out of his grasp.

"Just stay right here, okay?"

And she didn't realize until he'd gone, that he hadn't explained to her why one of his brothers might come outside in the middle of the night.

She scowled at the stable wall. But she waited, because she understood that even if she chafed at instruction, Landon really did want to keep her safe. And he wanted to solve this for her. Or maybe even with her. Still, she cheated a *little*.

She moved as quietly as she could to the edge of the stable so she could see around the building. In the distance, just a smudge of dark in the faded starlight, was her cabin. It was dark, as it should be. There was almost no movement. No breeze to flutter the grass or new leaves. The occasional whir of an insect or flapping sound of what was probably a bat could be heard, occasionally interrupted by the huff of a horse from inside the stables.

She nearly jumped a foot when she heard the rumble of voices. Coming from inside the stables. She strained to hear, but the words were muffled by the walls of the stables.

It had to be Landon talking to someone. Hopefully one of his brothers. But what if it wasn't? What if he was being confronted by the shooter from Mr. Field's house? What if they'd been followed and—

Hazeleigh sucked in a breath to calm herself. Landon knew how to handle things, and likely how to defend himself. Besides, the murmurs sounded calm. Still, she inched her way closer to the doors so she could make sure.

She *had* to make sure it was a Thompson. That Landon was safe. She knew he'd do the same in her position.

She kept moving as quietly as she could toward the open door, only stopping when she could finally make out the words.

"I'm not going to pretend like I didn't see you with Hazeleigh's horse that's been missing," someone said. Dunne, she thought. The low rasp. That emotionless way of speaking that he had. Still, it seemed odd he'd be out here. Because of a leg injury, he didn't ride horses unless he had to, and it *was* the middle of the night.

"I don't see why you couldn't," Landon replied, and his tone was genial enough. That teasing lilt he used when he was trying to get someone to his way of thinking without having an argument about it.

She wondered if it ever worked on his brothers. She'd certainly never seen any of them fall for it.

"Do you enjoy putting Zara through hell?"

Landon was very quiet for a *very* long moment that stretched out and made her own guilt settle heavy on her heart. She knew Zara would be worried about her, but…she just didn't see any other way.

"Didn't know you cared," Landon said at last, but there was no teasing lilt. His voice was almost as flat as Dunne's.

"What are you doing, Landon?"

Hazeleigh held her breath and waited for his answer. Because there had to be more to it than just *helping* her, didn't there?

But she didn't hear any answer, because an arm came around her from behind, pinning her arms to her side and propelling her forward.

LANDON HAD KNOWN this would be a mistake. Why had he come? Why had he let Hazeleigh come? He couldn't afford mistakes now, because Hazeleigh was the one who was going to pay for them.

But he stared at Dunne, trying not to let the pulsing anger out in his tone as he answered Dunne's question. "What I have to."

Before Dunne could argue with him, or express

more disappointment, Landon heard a noise. The *snick* of a footfall, and a squeak that could only be Hazeleigh.

He pushed past Dunne and out into the cool night air, hand on his gun as his heartbeat raced.

Then he sighed, irritably. Because it wasn't some nameless face holding Hazeleigh against her will.

It was his brother.

"It's her, Henry," Landon said, trying to keep the growl out of his tone. "Let her go."

It was dark, but he knew his brothers. How they moved. How they thought. He could recognize their shadows as well as he could recognize the back of his hand.

Hazeleigh wriggled, still in Henry's grasp, and Landon had to clench his hands into fists to keep himself from moving forward and lunging at his *brother*. "I said let her go."

"You're not in charge of me, Landon," Henry replied, his voice dark. But he was always dark. Henry had never fully learned to moderate the on-guard soldier in him.

Hazeleigh wriggled again. "This is ridiculous," she hissed. "Let me go right now."

Landon had to breathe very carefully. He'd learned to deal with his emotions, control them. Unlike Henry, he'd honed his military training and used it very rarely.

But few things tested that leash on his temper as the way Henry was holding onto Hazeleigh like she was some kind of common criminal. There was nothing he could say. If he moved…hell, if he *breathed* at this point, he was going to go after Henry.

As if sensing that, Henry let her go—slower than necessary—and dropped his arms. Still, he didn't step away. And Landon knew Dunne was standing behind him. Like they were at odds. Two against two.

"We'll go inside and talk this out," Dunne said, his voice devoid of anything except a flat kind of certainty. Two sides of a coin, really. The one with too much tension, the one with not enough.

And Landon, somewhere in the middle.

"I am *not* going inside," Hazeleigh said firmly. And she didn't stutter or hesitate like she might have a month or two ago if she'd been in a room alone with three of them.

It helped ease the apprehension inside of him. *Look at her. Coming into her own.*

He had to get her out of this confrontation with his brothers. "Hazeleigh needs to get a few things from her cabin."

"Hazeleigh needs to go inside and tell Zara she's all right. And then perhaps go to the cops and—"

"Zara knows I'm all right," Hazeleigh retorted. "She might be worried about me, but she knows I'm okay."

"Does she?" Dunne countered. "Because I'm pretty sure I'm the one who has been listening to her yell at everyone in her vicinity for the last two days."

"You wouldn't know how to read an emotion if it hit you over the head and said, 'Hi, I'm an emotion.'"

Landon and his brothers were struck dumb for a moment. Hazeleigh had just…been snotty and rude without even a fumble.

"Well," Henry said, the first one to break the last silence. "Who knew Hazeleigh had some fight in her."

"I do. And I'm doing this my way. I'm not putting you all in the middle of it. So you're going to go back inside and let me do what I need to do without telling *anyone.*"

"You put Landon in the middle of it," Dunne said darkly.

"He put himself in the middle of it," she returned.

Landon didn't interject. It was…amazing, watching her spar with Henry and Dunne. It was a shame that it was murder and false accusations that had gotten her to this point, but it was still a sight to behold.

But his brothers turned to him in the inky dark, clearly wanting his verdict.

"I think we all know the cops can't help. Not until we have some better proof that Hazeleigh wasn't involved. And I think we all know that as much as Zara would feel some relief knowing Hazeleigh is safe and sound, she would not handle the information in a way that would allow us to be *subtle.*"

Henry snorted a little. "All the subtlety of a freight train."

"Exactly. Hazeleigh needs to get into her cabin and grab a few things. Then she'll go back into hiding."

"With you?"

"Not *with* me," Landon replied. "I'm helping her with access to a few things. Information."

"Someone shot at you," Dunne pointed out. "That scratch wasn't an accident. So why not go to the cops and—"

"No," Hazeleigh said firmly. "I know you all don't trust me, or think I'm just some—" she was clearly struggling to find the words "—weak-willed, scaredy-cat, foolish…whatever. You aren't the first, likely won't be the last, but I know one thing. I cannot go to the cops."

"I've never thought you were *foolish*," Henry muttered in return.

Landon barely resisted the urge to punch him in the nose. But Hazeleigh kept talking.

"It's important that I clear my name before we go to them. It's important to figure out who's trying to frame me. I might be the *only* one who can determine who killed Mr. Field—particularly if the police think I did it and won't listen to me about what I know about Mr. Field's life. I can't quite do it on my own, and Landon has inserted himself in the whole thing to help. And I appreciate that help. Now, I'm going to ask for yours. Pretend you never saw me. Please."

Landon didn't know how anyone could ever say no to that request, and both Dunne and Henry shifted uncomfortably—very rare indeed.

"All right," Dunne agreed after a long silence. "But not forever. You've got a leash, Landon. Three more days. Tops."

Henry huffed out an irritated breath. "Forty-eight hours, then we barge in. Take it or leave it."

"I preferred Dunne's deal," Hazeleigh replied.

"Tough."

Hazeleigh sighed and though it was dark, he got the feeling she was studying him. Considering…everything. "Fine," she said after a moment or two. "Forty-eight hours."

"You better come inside with us," Dunne said to Landon. "Jake's going to notice something's off, and even if he *would* keep something from Zara, I think we all know he can't. So you'll need to come in and pretend to go to bed."

"I'm not leaving Hazeleigh out here alone."

"It's okay," Hazeleigh said. "You go inside. I'll go to my cabin and get what I need."

Landon took her arm in the dark, pulled her away from Henry and Dunne, but before he could say anything, she was already pleading her case.

"I can do it myself, Landon. I'll get the laptop and meet you back behind the stables. I promise, I won't go anywhere without you."

"Hazeleigh…"

"I can do it, Landon." She grabbed his hands. Squeezed. "I have to do it."

It went against every instinct he had. But he couldn't refuse her. "All right," he muttered. "Fifteen minutes, then I come after you."

"It won't take me more than ten," she assured him. Then she dropped his hands, and began to walk through the dark, toward her cabin.

Landon watched her go—just a shadow—and still it felt wrong. Bone-deep wrong.

Henry clapped him on the shoulder, hard, and didn't let go as he practically pushed Landon toward the house. "We've got a *lot* to discuss, brother."

"Don't have time for discussions." He'd go inside, make a joke, then go straight to bed. Then out the window and over to the cabin. He looked over his shoulder as Henry pushed him to the porch.

She shouldn't be out there alone in the dark.

"Shocks the hell out of me, but seems like maybe Hazeleigh can handle herself," Dunne said.

Maybe. No—no maybes. Landon knew she could.

But that didn't make the clutching terror of worry loosen in his gut.

Chapter Fifteen

Hazeleigh walked confidently across the front yard she'd spent her entire life walking across. During the day. At night. Barefoot. Bundled up for a blizzard. Every Hart going back one hundred and fifty years had done the same. Tragedy. Triumph.

Now her.

She would be brave. She would be strong. She'd held her own—not just with Landon, but with Henry *and* Dunne. Truth be told, they were the two Thompson brothers she found the most intimidating.

Funny, because she knew they *all* looked to Cal as kind of a de facto leader. She supposed it was some oldest-brother thing, but still, for all Cal's scowls and dour proclamations, he didn't have the same edge Henry and Dunne did.

Henry in particular.

No, she'd never felt comfortable around Henry, but back there she hadn't *shown* it. She'd hidden her nerves away behind bravado and the driving need to do just this.

She walked around to the back of her cabin, weaved through the gardens she loved to tend in the summer.

"I'll be home soon," she whispered. A promise to her plants *and* herself.

She paused at the door and looked out over the yard to the big house. There was a light on in the kitchen window. She didn't see anyone lurking around the house, so assumed Landon and his brothers had already gone inside.

There was the familiar pang for all that had been lost. Her mother. Amberleigh. Her childhood. Mr. Field and the job she'd loved.

Hazeleigh swallowed at the lump in her throat. Mr. Field was the only one who'd ever *needed* her. Now he was gone.

She closed her eyes and breathed deeply. In the dark she made a promise to him, too. *I'll find out who did this. No matter what it takes.*

The nonexistent breeze picked up for a moment, and for a fleeting, crazy second she thought she smelled peppermints—the kind Mr. Field always had on hand.

Silly.

She pulled her keys out of her pocket and unlocked the back door, stepping immediately into her kitchen. Everything was still and quiet. It smelled…stale. Like old coffee and…other people.

The cops had no doubt searched it. Gone through her things and… She couldn't think about it. It wasn't the first time.

The first time they had found something much worse: evidence against her.

She was pretty sure they hadn't found anything this time because Dunne or Henry surely would have said something. Or Landon would have found out and said something.

So if someone was trying to frame her, at least they hadn't planted evidence in her cabin. *That* was something. Something she'd hold on to.

She closed the door behind her very carefully, making every effort to make no noise—not even a squeak. She didn't flip on the lights. She stood, trying to remember where she would have left her laptop.

She took it everywhere—worked from bed, from the couch in the living room, from the kitchen table. When she was deep in research or organization mode, she thought of little else. But the last time she'd been home…

It had been the morning of Mr. Field's murder. She'd woken up, checked her phone, seen his message. Which meant her laptop was probably still in her bedroom, as she'd been working from bed the night before.

She took a deep breath to settle her nerves, and then carefully began to move. The cabin was dark, but she knew where everything was, and her eyes had adjusted. It wasn't the first time she'd tiptoed through the cabin in the pitch-black. At times, Hazeleigh woke in the middle of the night, parched from some terrible nightmare and needing a drink of water or some fresh night air. When Zara had still been her roommate, Hazeleigh had always kept the lights off as she made her way through the cabin.

So this was old hat. Everything was fine and safe, and she would get the laptop and meet Landon at the stables.

She'd figure this out. And she'd do it in *thirty-six*

darn hours. Just to prove Henry—Mr. Forty-eight Hours—and his bad attitude wrong.

She liked that. Having a sense of purpose. Having an enemy with a face, even if it was Landon's brother and he wasn't really her enemy. Just kind of a meanie. Maybe not even that. Maybe he was simply mad that Landon was wrapped up in something that might get him in trouble, and was blaming her.

Could she blame Henry for that?

She puffed out a breath. She had to focus on finding the laptop. Leave everything else behind. She moved through the kitchen in the dark, easily avoiding the small kitchen table and feeling her way down the hall until she reached her bedroom.

She considered turning on the light, since the only window in her room faced away from the main house, but that would be an unnecessary risk. She'd just have to sit down on the bed and paw around for the laptop where she usually set it on the ground, between her bed and her nightstand.

And she'd need her cord, which she usually kept out in the living room. She muttered a curse under her breath. She'd told Landon she'd be ten minutes, and so far she was moving about as quickly as molasses.

She sat on the bed, reached down to where she usually kept her laptop. Her hand clasped over the cool metal. *Success.* She picked it up and clutched it to her chest. Now she just needed the cord.

She moved to the living room, felt around on the ground until she touched the cord. She unplugged it and then…

She straightened, then stilled. Had she…heard something? A creak? A rustle? Her heart leaped into her throat.

It might just be Landon. Maybe her time was up, and he'd gotten worried, but one of her old bad feelings overwhelmed her.

She lurched forward, suddenly sure she had to get out of there. But her shin banged against her coffee table and she narrowly swallowed down a yelp of pain as she hopped on one leg.

She stilled, tried to get her breathing under control, and *listened*. She waited and waited and waited and waited.

Nothing happened. There was no sound. No one jumping out—friend or foe. There was nothing.

Silly, Hazeleigh. Your feelings are wrong and pointless and you should stop thinking there could ever actually be something inside of you that might actually have any sense of what's going on around you.

She swallowed down her emotional response to the nasty voice in her head. It wasn't true. As unreliable as her feelings could be, they did occasionally help.

Just sometimes, they were very far off the mark. Or maybe… Maybe someone else was in danger. Usually she had a sense of who. She'd saved Zara more than once from a bad accident, though maybe twice in a lifetime wasn't enough to really count on.

But she *had* been right. She'd known about Amberleigh—had a sick, horrible feeling just like now, before Zara had accidentally dug up their sister's body.

Maybe Zara was in trouble. Maybe Landon was…

No, he was with his brothers, and so was Zara. Maybe they were simply arguing or something else had given her a bad feeling. Hardly as serious as the end of any-one's life.

She blew out a breath and moved forward. Every-thing was fine, or as fine as it could be, and if some-one out there was having something terrible happen to them, well, that was a shame, but there wasn't much she could do about it unless her "feeling" decided to give her more information.

She moved to the kitchen, pausing once more to lis-ten for noises, but she heard nothing out of the ordinary. The bad feeling was still churning around in her chest, but she didn't know what to do with it. No one was in here with her, and she'd gotten what she'd come for.

She licked her lips, swallowed at her dry throat, then opened the kitchen door. She stepped back into the night air, her garden. Down the stairs, a few steps across the pathway and into the yard. Landon was likely already waiting for her behind the stables.

God, she hoped so.

But before she made it, arms came around her from behind, a too-tight hold that had the laptop and cord clattering into the grass.

"Let me go, Henry." But she knew, even as she said it, that it wasn't Henry. Or Landon. Or Dunne. It was a stranger.

"We knew you'd come," the voice said, and she strug-gled to recognize it, but there was absolutely nothing familiar about it.

LANDON BIT BACK impatience with himself. He hated leaving Hazeleigh alone, but he knew his brothers. He had to do this or they wouldn't even give him the allotted forty-eight hours.

Forty-eight hours wasn't enough, even with the leads they'd gotten today. He needed more time. Hazeleigh needed more time.

Landon took a seat at the kitchen table and smiled blandly at Cal.

Everything would be fine. Hazeleigh knew her way around her cabin. It was the middle of the night and there were no cops hanging around.

Everything was fine.

He closed his hand into a fist under the table. Nothing felt fine.

Dunne also sat at the kitchen table. Henry paced. Cal stood stock-still.

"Going to call in the rest of the cavalry or can we let this slide, fellas?"

Dunne sighed. Henry all but growled.

"I don't think we need to include anyone else," Cal said evenly, after a time. "But you should know better than to sneak around here with *her* when Jake could have easily been the one to find you."

They all looked at the kitchen entrance like just mentioning Jake might make him appear. He didn't, but the thought that he would made Landon feel guilty. Although, he wouldn't be sitting here worrying about guilt if Henry and Dunne had minded their own damn business.

"So what can we do?" Cal said.

Henry and Dunne both shot Cal surprised glances, immediately hidden away. Then they turned to Landon. Because the three of them preferred pretending like they were still in the military. Like Cal was the leader and they were on some kind of mission.

Landon had understood at first, but the more Jake and Brody settled into *real* actual lives, the more he wanted that. Not just because being a soldier had been taken away from him, but because they seemed... happy.

These three? Not so much.

But they wanted to help, and Landon wished he knew how he could use their skills to figure this out.

"We're following some leads. I'm not sure there's anything you can do." Landon remembered Hazeleigh's story about the little girl. He related it to the men. "I don't think it can connect. What would a little girl wandering around on her own have to do with Mr. Field's murder?"

"Nothing, on the surface," Henry said.

"But we all know better than to believe the surface," Dunne added.

"We'll see what we can figure out about the girl." Cal's frown deepened. "A kid shouldn't be running around on her own out here. Especially on land that's supposed to be deserted."

"Hazeleigh had the same concerns. But she said she seemed...okay. Capable. Hazeleigh told her she was Zara, so another thing to keep Jake out of."

"They keep adding up," Cal muttered.

"I don't like it either," Landon said. "But it has to be done."

"For now," Cal replied. "I'm with you on this, but I'm with Henry, too. If you can't get it done in forty-

eight hours, we've got to pull the plug. Before someone gets hurt."

"Hazeleigh being arrested is someone getting hurt."

Cal held his gaze. "Maybe she thinks that, but it's
hardly the end of the world. And it's happened to her
before and she survived."

"Yeah, because we got her out of it. Jake and the rest
of us. So how about instead of expecting a woman who
has never had anything to do with murder or war to
suck it up and deal with jail, we get this done."

"You're emotionally involved," Cal said, sounding
shocked. Disappointment was threaded through the
three simple words.

It took way too much effort to keep his voice low,
but he wasn't going to deny it. No matter how little Cal
approved of him being *emotionally involved*. "You're
damn right I am."

"What is it with you three?" Henry muttered dis-
gustedly. "You can't help someone without falling in
love?"

Love felt…heavy. A bit much, a bridge too far. But
he wasn't about to argue semantics for being emotionally involved at the moment. "The bottom line is she
needs help, and I can give it. Take emotions out of it.
It needs to be done."

"But you can't take emotions out of it. You have
them."

"So what? Who said being detached and unemo-
tional was the be-all end-all? Here we are, washed-up
soldiers who had to be wiped off the grid not because
we got too emotional or invested, but because some
computer tech pushed the wrong damn button."

No one moved. No one said anything. Because it was true, but maybe not a truth any of them had really considered. Had maybe even *avoided* considering.

Landon stood. "I don't want her out there alone longer than she has to be," he said quietly, but with enough venom to keep anyone else from arguing. "We'll do our best to figure this out in forty-eight hours. We have a lead. We have something to go on. But I need you to remember she isn't *us*. She isn't a soldier. She has a family and a life that was already upended— by her dad selling this place to us, by her sister being dead and buried on our land and her getting blamed for it for a time. Now her boss is dead, and she found the body. She might be stronger and braver than we've given her credit for, but she's not an automaton like we were. She's a person."

"Quite a speech."

Landon didn't turn around, but he did close his eyes and let out a long sigh. "How much of that did you hear?"

"More than I wanted to," Jake replied. "Landon, I can't—"

"Then don't," Landon said, cutting him off. He moved for the exit. He wasn't going to sit around and talk about this anymore. "Do whatever you guys need to do. Me? I'm done talking about what I'm *going* to do. I'm going to go do it."

He pushed passed Jake. Luckily none of his brothers tried to stop him. Maybe they'd come after him. Maybe they'd let him handle this. He genuinely didn't care at this moment, because he couldn't take another second of Hazeleigh being out there alone. She was likely waiting for him.

But when he got to the stables, Hazeleigh wasn't there.

And the terrible feeling he hadn't been able to shake intensified.

Chapter Sixteen

Hazeleigh wanted to fall apart, but she knew everyone around her was in danger if she did. Her sister was in the house, just a short distance away. Kate. Landon and all his brothers. If the man had a gun, and someone came running...

The thought swept through her in a shudder. So she stood very still while this man held on to her...too tightly.

She swallowed down the revulsion of being pressed to some stranger's fleshy body.

"Who are you?" she asked, though her voice wavered. Not quite the show of strength she'd wanted.

"You don't know?" He laughed in her ear, his hot breath fluttering her hair. She wanted to wretch.

Instead, she kept holding herself still. Landon would come and get her. He would know something was wrong. He'd known when Henry had grabbed her. Certainly he'd know things were amiss and he'd...fix them. He wouldn't barge in. He'd sneak in. He wouldn't get shot.

Not again.

In the meantime, she'd do everything she could to remain unhurt and right here.

"Pick up the computer," the man said. "You try to run, the whole house goes up in flames."

Hazeleigh remained absolutely still. The statement had cold shock moving through her. The house. Did he mean her cabin, or…?

"And not just fire. I mean the whole thing explodes. Won't be too many survivors. How many people in there, you think? Seven? Or is it eight now?"

He meant the big house. "How would you do that?"

He laughed again. His hot breath close to her ear. "You think any of this was spur-of-the-moment? We've been planning it all. Bit by bit. Now, you're coming with me."

"This doesn't make any sense," she muttered. And who was *we*?

"Of course it doesn't. To someone as stupid as *you*."

Without thinking, she jerked her arm. An instinctual retaliation. He held firm, jerked her back just as hard, if not harder. It sent a shock of pain down her arm, and she made a noise of distress.

He jerked her again, even harder. "Shut up or I'll have to kill all of you."

"You're *hurting* me."

"I haven't even started hurting you. Pick up the computer. Shut the hell up and let's go."

"If you take me, they'll know," Hazeleigh said desperately. "And the police will know I didn't kill Mr. Field, because I've been kidnapped. If you shoot me, you don't have a scapegoat for Mr. Field's murder."

He was quiet for a moment, studying her. "Who would know I took you? You ran away on your own. Pretty dumb if you ask me."

She didn't want to give up Landon's identity since this man didn't seem to know about his involvement. So this man hadn't been following her. Had just been sitting at her cabin, waiting. She had to use what he didn't know against him. "You think I've been avoiding the cops on my own? You think I came here in the middle of the night *alone*?" She thought about mentioning Mr. Field's house, but she didn't know enough. Was this man working alone? Was he the same man who'd shot at them?

He knew enough to know where she lived. He knew enough about her to wait and—

"Pick up the computer and give it to me. Or they explode." He loosened his grip a little, so she could crouch and reach for it with one arm.

Hazeleigh let out a shaky breath. She would try to bide her time and keep the man right here, where Landon would find them. She kneeled. Took a breath. Picked up the laptop.

"Come *on*."

She slowly stood, and he pulled on her arm again. A hard, bruising grasp.

She had to think. He was big. The top of her head just barely came up to his chin. His hand on her arm was meaty.

He ripped the laptop out of her grasp.

"You won't be able to get what you're looking for without my passwords." She had no idea what he was after—but if he was after what *she* was after…

The guy snorted. "That's why you're coming with me." He started dragging her, and she realized if he held her *and* the computer, there was no hand free for him to somehow set off the explosives.

So she fought. She kicked. She wrenched her arm from every angle she could think of as he tried to pull her. The man grunted and fought right back, holding her firm.

But the house didn't explode, so that was something.

Then she heard her name shouted from a distance. *Landon.*

She didn't have time to think—she could only act. With one well-placed kick, she managed to free herself from the would-be kidnapper's tight grasp as he let out a gasp of pain.

She managed one step toward Landon's voice before the man grabbed her by the hair. He ripped her backward. Pain exploded all over her scalp and she stopped fighting as a protective measure.

"Tell him to back off, or everyone inside dies," he hissed into her ear.

Hazeleigh had to marshal all her emotions, all her thoughts. She knew she was taking too long when the man yanked her hair again. She gasped in pain.

"Hazeleigh." It was Landon's voice. Too far away. But calm. Deadly calm. In the darkness. "Don't move."

"Tell him," the man said. Odd that he wouldn't call out to Landon himself.

Hazeleigh managed to clear her throat. "He—he says he has explosives in the basement."

Landon laughed. Actually laughed. "My ass."

"That house isn't watched twenty-four-seven," the man whispered again.

Hazeleigh reiterated his words to Landon. She couldn't see anyone, but she assumed some of the brothers were out there as well. *Please.*

"No, but it's full of six men who'd know if it was broken into. Why are you lying? And so badly?"

All of a sudden, the man dropped her. She kneeled in the grass, utterly confused, pain radiating over her scalp. But she could hear his retreating footsteps, and then footsteps approaching her.

There were hands on her. All over her. But it was Landon. Maybe Dunne. Checking her to make sure she was okay.

"He has my computer."

"Not important," Landon said sharply.

"It *is* important. All the information we—"

Landon spoke, like he wasn't even listening to her. "Dunne, sweep the basement. He claimed he put explosives there."

"My ass," Dunne muttered, but he hurried away to check.

"Cal, Henry, Jake, go after him. Don't lose him."

"Landon—"

But Cal spoke over her trying to speak. "Brody and Jake are already on it, Henry not far behind. We'll spread out, make a circle. You should stay here."

"Don't lose him," Landon said, and then Cal was gone, too.

Landon scooped her up like she couldn't walk herself. She pushed at his chest. "I'm fine. I'm okay."

"We're getting you inside," he said grimly. Sternly. "And you're not leaving my sight."

LANDON CARRIED HAZELEIGH the whole way inside. So much for keeping everyone out of this. So much for—

The terror he'd felt raged so high it had turned to a frigid cold, and as he didn't trust that feeling, he said nothing. Did nothing. He called on that old robotic-soldier facade to make it inside with her. He carried her to the couch and carefully deposited her.

What Landon really wanted to do was take after the man who'd had his hands on Hazeleigh, but he knew he couldn't. Not because Hazeleigh needed him, but because it wouldn't end well for the man. And while that didn't matter in the least to him, they needed information. They did not need Landon to exact revenge.

Landon took a step back from the couch, looking down at Hazeleigh critically. She was a little pale, but otherwise not too worse for wear.

The man had touched her. Tried to kidnap her. And a few more minutes…

He swallowed against his anger over the situation clogging his throat. "Are you hurt?" he asked.

She blinked, eyebrows drawing together as if she was confused by the question. "No, not—"

"What is going—" Zara appeared from the kitchen. Apparently she hadn't known about what had gone on outside, and that it involved Hazeleigh, because her eyes widened, she dropped the dish towel she'd been strangling and rushed over to Hazeleigh, then threw her arms around her sister.

Hazeleigh put an arm around Zara, but her eyes remained on his. That same confusion in the brown depths.

Zara looked up at him next, and while Hazeleigh's

gaze was soft, if confused, Zara's was squinted and angry. "What the hell is going on?" she demanded of him.

But Hazeleigh put a hand on one of Zara's. "Where's Kate?"

"She wasn't feeling well. Probably sleeping through it all. I'll catch her up in the morning, or Brody will. Now, if you avoid my question one more time…"

Hazeleigh sighed, looking down at her hand over her sister's. Landon looked at their hands, too. He shouldn't be here. He didn't *belong* here. Why'd he think he was the one to step in and fix things?

"I snuck back to my cabin," Hazeleigh explained, clearly leaving out his involvement in the situation. "I wanted my computer. I thought maybe I could figure out some things if I had my computer. I could read Mr. Field's emails and such. But someone was at the cabin waiting for me." Her gaze returned to Landon. "Whoever it was had been waiting for me for a long time."

She was trying to absolve him. That he couldn't have known simply because the man had been waiting. Which made the cold inside of him branch out. Douse more molten-hot fury. He had to freeze it out. If he didn't…

Because he'd known something was wrong, and he'd ignored it. He'd known leaving her alone was wrong, but he'd done it.

There was no absolution to be had. Every choice from the beginning had been wrong. Because he'd let emotion and his own ego sway him. Just like Cal had always warned them.

"Why?" Zara asked, still clutching on to Hazeleigh as if her sister might disappear again.

"Whoever it was wanted information. I think… Zara, I know this sounds crazy, but I think this all ties to Mr. Field's research. This man who'd been waiting wanted my computer. The only thing he could want is access to Mr. Field's research on the bank robbery."

"Fake bank robbery, Haze. Who cares about some old myth?"

"Someone, I think. Maybe I'm wrong, but…" She snuck another glance at Landon. But he could neither move nor speak. Not without shattering.

"Okay, so you have a lead. Take it to the police and—"

Hazeleigh withdrew herself from Zara's grasp. "No."

"Haze—"

"I won't. I can't. Not until we can prove someone else did it. We need evidence. I just… I had this feeling, Zara. Bone-deep. I can't go back to jail. Or even a holding cell or whatever. I just know the police can't help me. I *know* it."

Zara sighed, but she didn't argue with Hazeleigh.

"Dunne's checking the house," Landon said, but his voice sounded like little more than a rasp. "The rest of them are on the guy's tail. If they catch him, we'll call the police. Go from there."

Hazeleigh frowned. "He didn't kill Mr. Field. Whoever it is, he's involved, but he didn't kill Mr. Field."

"How do you know that?" Zara asked before Landon could.

"He's not working alone. He said *we*, and he talked about planning. And he just… He didn't strike me as very smart. Or at least, he thought I was…" She trailed off, looked at Zara, then at him.

Landon didn't know what she was about to say, what she wanted to hide, but he had the sneaking suspicion she was trying to save him from Zara's wrath. Or maybe Jake's.

At the moment, he wanted everyone's wrath. He wanted nothing but anger and blame and guilt and anything dark. Because that's what he deserved for these missteps and failures.

"Tell her the whole truth," Landon said flatly.

She closed her eyes as if in pain. "Landon."

"What's the whole truth?" Zara demanded.

Hazeleigh plastered a smile on her face and took Zara's hand in hers. "Landon's been helping me."

Zara shot to her feet, but Hazeleigh held firm. Landon supposed it kept him from getting a punch in the nose, but he wouldn't have minded that right now.

"You've been *lying* to me? To Jake?"

"I begged him to," Hazeleigh said before Landon could say something that might make Zara angrier. "And you'll be relieved to know Landon was the one who convinced me not to run away completely. He thought we could figure out who did this, clear my name. And we're making progress."

"Progress," Landon scoffed. "You were almost kidnapped."

"But I wasn't," she returned firmly. She was far more calm than he was, which was wrong. She should be shaken up. Afraid. As damn terrified as he was underneath it all.

Instead, she seemed to have it all figured out and he

wanted to *shake* her. The man inside her cabin could
have shot her dead. Done. The end. Because Landon
had let her go alone.

"And that's why I think this guy wasn't very smart,"
Hazeleigh continued, maddeningly casual. "I kept slowing things down. Talking to him. Taking my time. Because I knew you'd come, and…"

The rest of her words were lost to the buzzing in
his head. *I knew you'd come.* But he hadn't come soon
enough. He should have. The minute he'd felt something was wrong. Instead he'd sat in the kitchen *chat-
ting* with his brothers. As if talking ever got the job
done. As if their approval or support mattered when
Hazeleigh had been in trouble.

Knowing he'd come.

"Landon." She stood and reached for him, but he
stepped away before her hand could take his. Something once so rare that had now become almost a habit.

He'd crumble if she touched him now. Into dust.
"Zara, keep an eye on her. I'm—"

The screen door behind him squeaked open and Jake
popped his head in.

"We've got him," Jake said. He eyed Hazeleigh and
Zara. "Brought him into Henry's shed. We thought
you'd want to question him yourself."

"Yes, I do," Landon said. "I'll be there in a minute."

Whether Jake sensed the tension in the room or just
didn't want to face Zara's inevitable wrath quite yet, he
nodded and disappeared back into the night.

Landon turned to the sisters. He held his hands behind his back, spread his feet. *At ease, soldier.* Sometimes a man needed to be a soldier and nothing else.

"This is what's going to happen," Landon said, and he knew how stiff he sounded. How stiff he must look considering how frozen he felt. And it might have amused him any other time, as he realized how much he sounded and probably looked like Cal.

Maybe after all this was over, he'd understand Cal better. But for now, he could only focus on himself. On surviving. On making this as right as he could for Hazeleigh, even though he'd failed miserably tonight. "You will stay right here. We will question this guy. If it's enough to call in the cops, we will."

"If it's not?" Hazeleigh demanded, sparks of temper in her eyes. The sisters looked especially alike in the moment. Hazeleigh in his sweatshirt, even if she was wearing her skirt. Zara rumpled in sweats and a T-shirt.

"We'll decide what's next," Landon said in a tone that brooked no argument.

Somehow, Hazeleigh found one. "By *we* you mean you and me?"

"No, I mean my brothers and I." He turned toward the door.

"Landon." Her voice was very direct. Very serious. And he had no choice but to stop, turn and meet her gaze. "You will not bulldoze me," she said. "None of you. You may have crashed in, you may have helped, but at the end of the day it's *my* life on the line."

There was such a complicated tangle of emotions inside of him that he simply didn't trust himself to speak. Her life on the line—which might have been over. So easily.

And it would have been his fault.

So he said nothing and left her with her sister.

Chapter Seventeen

Hazeleigh stood and watched him not respond, just...
leave. She didn't understand what had happened, what
had changed. Why had he gotten so cold? She'd never
seen him like that.

It made her want to cry, and she wasn't even sure
why. But crying and wringing her hands had gotten
her nowhere.

Instead, she focused on all the frustration she felt inside. Better than sadness. Better than all the fear she'd
felt when that man had grabbed her.

"Can you believe him? *We'll* question him. *We'll*
call the police." She fumed. "*I'm* the one wanted for
murder. And he's just sweeping in. Taking over. *Telling*
me what to do." Hazeleigh began to pace. She wanted
to break something. She wanted to...

She caught Zara staring at her with a slightly open-
mouthed expression. "What?"

"I've never seen you like this," Zara said softly.
"Never."

Hazeleigh stopped pacing. "Well, no one's ever tried
to kidnap me before."

"Maybe not, but you've been suspected of murder

before. You've been manhandled before. Dad was always a high-handed jerk to you. And you always…"

Hazeleigh looked down at her hands. She knew what she always did. Cowered. Hid. Heaped a bunch of self-blame on herself. She sucked in a breath and met Zara's gaze. "I don't want to be that person anymore."

Zara finally stood from the couch. She stood in front of Hazeleigh, looking strangely…moved. She even reached out and took Hazeleigh's hands in hers. "Good." But Zara studied her face, as if still looking for that old cowardly behavior.

"Zara…" She didn't know what she wanted to say. Or she didn't have the words. Things had changed. And it wasn't just all of a sudden. It was like…all paths she'd been on the last few months had led her here. To a place where she could finally grab on to a…new self.

No, not new. Someone who'd grown out of bad things and bad habits and was determined to find something stronger within herself. Something braver. So she could face…well, everything she was up against now.

She had to face it. Whatever was going on with Landon couldn't influence *her*. This was *her* life, and she appreciated his help—she didn't want him to stop *helping*. She just couldn't stand the thought of him sweeping in and taking over, leaving her here to wring her hands.

She looked down at her hands, caught in Zara's, who was not the touchy sort. But she held on.

There was no ring where there should have been though. Hazeleigh frowned. "Don't tell me you said no."

Zara's expression scrunched into confusion as she looked down at their hands. "No to what?"

Hazeleigh realized her mistake. Because, of *course*, Jake wasn't going to propose while Zara was worried over her sister being on the run. "Erm…"

Zara tugged her hands away. She laughed, but there was a little hint of panic behind it. "You don't mean…" She shook her head. "You're being ridiculous."

But she wasn't. And… Well, it was kind of nice to watch someone else freak out about something in the midst of her own problems. "I helped him pick out the ring. I told him I thought you were ready. I hope I wasn't wrong."

"A ring," Zara echoed, as if Hazeleigh had said something like *poison*.

"I suppose I ruined the timing of things when I ran away," Hazeleigh said. "I am sorry for that. Although I guess it's more Mr. Field's murderer's fault." Because not everything was her fault. She didn't need to blame herself for everything that happened, just like Landon had told her.

"I…" Zara blinked, completely speechless.

A feat indeed.

"I hope you'll pretend to be surprised when this is all over and he does ask." Hazeleigh had to bite back a grin. It was so rare to see Zara off the mark that even with everything going on around them, Hazeleigh enjoyed it. "I'd hate to be the reason the moment was ruined."

"Ruined?" Zara seemed to get a hold of herself, though she had her fist pressed to her heart like she was trying to keep it from exploding through her chest. "No, I think… I think I'm glad I had some forewarning."

"You think?"

Zara looked up at Hazeleigh. "He really wants to *marry* me?" she whispered. Even though they *lived* together. And Zara still seemed uncertain. Not about Jake's feelings so much as…the future.

It was like something clicking into place for Hazeleigh. She'd always fancied Zara the strong one, and her the weak one. But…people—all people—were far more complicated than that.

No matter how strong. How weak. Life was a series of challenges, and sometimes you met them with mistakes. But sometimes…wonderful things happened. She was ready for some wonderful things.

"Of course he does. He loves you. You make each other happy." Hazeleigh smiled at her sister. "Zara, you've never been so happy. Don't overthink it."

Zara swallowed. "But…"

"No *buts*."

"This is ridiculous," Zara said, shaking her head vigorously. "Why are we talking about this in the middle of the night while those six imbeciles take care of everything?"

"I don't know. They really are imbeciles, aren't they?"

"Honorable, wonderful imbeciles, but imbeciles nonetheless," Zara said with a sharp nod. She opened her mouth, and Hazeleigh knew she was about to outline a plan. Take over. Be in charge.

But Hazeleigh realized for the first time that it was her job to do that. "I need to talk to that man who tried to kidnap me. I need to get to the bottom of it, so we can all get on with our lives."

"So we'll go barge in there and demand to ask your questions."

Hazeleigh blinked. "What?"

"You don't have to sit here. You don't have to wait around, and you don't have to run. You can fight. You can do what *you* think is right. The Thompson brothers might be a muscly, loudmouthed group of bossy imbeciles, but they're going to have to bodily remove us if they don't like your plan."

Your plan. Why did that feel so good? But she thought about Landon carrying her all the way from the cabin to the house no matter how she'd protested. "I think Landon might bodily remove me right now."

Zara studied her carefully. "Yeah, he just might." And Hazeleigh got the distinct feeling Zara understood that maybe something was happening there. But then she shrugged it all away easily enough. "I'll fight him, you ask your questions. Teamwork."

It was ridiculous. The idea of Zara going in there, fighting Landon, while Hazeleigh faced her attempted kidnapper and asked questions. It wouldn't go down that way. But Zara was right.

The brothers might be bossy and controlling when they thought they were doing the right thing, but they weren't going to…just toss her out.

They'd try. They'd argue, but if she pleaded her case, especially to Landon, he'd cave. When it came to her, he seemed to always cave. "I can do it. I can fight him," she decided. Maybe not with fists. But with reason. And emotion.

"I'm still coming with."

"Shouldn't I do it on my own? I can do it on my own. It's time I… Well, stand on my own two feet, I guess."

"You can be strong and stand on your own two feet *and* have support, Haze. It isn't all one or the other."

"Since when do you think that, Miss Independent?" Hazeleigh asked with a smile, though she knew the answer before Zara even said it.

Zara wrinkled her nose. "I guess since Jake," she said, sounding embarrassed. But Hazeleigh didn't think it was anything to be embarrassed about.

It was beautiful.

Jake and Zara deserved more of their happily-ever-after. And Hazeleigh deserved a little of her own. Which meant, they had to end this. "Let's go."

It irritated Landon that Hazeleigh's estimation was right. The man who'd tried to kidnap her wasn't smart. He was capable of killing, maybe, but not of killing a man and framing someone else, all the while having some deeper plan clearly in place.

Not that the would-be kidnapper knew the plan. Oh, he thought he did, but the more questions he was asked, the more he seemed to realize how little he really did know.

Which made him mad. He fought against where he was tied to the chair. Seemingly not thinking through that even if he did get free—which he wouldn't—he'd have to get through *six* trained ex-military men.

"What's with the explosives talk?" Dunne asked when it was clear they weren't getting anywhere with a name for the alleged murderer. "I went through the whole house and there wasn't anything."

"Had to get her to come with me without screaming, didn't I?"

Landon's hands curled into fists. He took a step toward the man without even realizing it.

"Why not knock her out? Drug her? A million ways to take her." Henry said it flippantly, but Landon could picture those possibilities all too clearly. As if that's what had actually happened.

"You're right about that." The guy grinned, licked his lips. "A million ways to take her!" Then he laughed, like he expected them all to join in the joke.

Landon's fist unclenched, but only enough to land on the gun still on his hip. He could end it right here. No questions asked.

Cal stepped between him and the man. For a second, Cal's face was unfocused and Landon had to blink to see. Past the need for revenge and payback for hurting Hazeleigh. Past the thudding violence inside of him.

Like father, like son.

"Stand down, Landon."

"You're not my commanding officer anymore." Because maybe this was just who he was and trying to be someone else all these years was pointless.

"No," Cal said evenly. Then he reached out and put his hand on Landon's shoulder. Squeezed. "I'm your brother. Step outside."

Landon didn't know what it was, but whatever was locked tight eased, and though he didn't step outside himself, he did let Cal lead him outside. Henry and Jake followed.

"What do we do with this bozo?" Henry asked.

"We can't let him go. Dumb or not, he's a danger," Jake replied. "And not just to Hazeleigh."

No, they were all involved now. What a mess.

"Speak of the devil," Henry muttered.

Landon looked up to see Hazeleigh and Zara step out onto the porch. It was still dark, but someone had flipped on the porch light, and they were two dimly lit shadows as they marched across the yard.

She *was* a devil. His own personal Satan. Because he hadn't made mistakes until she'd come around. Even now he simply wanted to bundle her up and hold her and make this bad stuff all go away.

She stopped in front of him, and even though he had the impression she was trying to pose her demand to all of them, she held his gaze and his alone.

"I need to talk to that man."

"No." Landon was gratified that Henry and Cal's *no's* echoed with his even if his was overloud in his ears.

Jake's *no* was missing, but Landon could only assume that Jake would play traitor and be on Zara's side for this.

"I did not request permission," she said firmly. "Move." She raised an eyebrow. First at Landon. Then at Jake.

None of his brothers moved.

"What's the harm of her asking some questions?" Zara demanded. "She might think to ask something your brain trust doesn't."

"Did it ever occur to you to ask nicely, Zara?" Jake muttered.

"Why don't you tell us your questions and we'll ask him," Cal suggested. It was reasonable enough.

Hazeleigh's mouth firmed. "Open the door, Landon."

"I'm not your lapdog, Hazeleigh."

For a second, hurt flashed through her expression.

But all that emotion had gotten them nothing but trouble. He couldn't give in to it.

She turned to Cal. "You seem to be the de facto leader around here, and I appreciate all that you and your brothers have done or tried to do for me, but the fact of the matter is I am the one being framed for murder. *I* am the one who almost got kidnapped. I feel like I'm owed a little face time with the man who wanted to take me and my laptop against my will."

Landon watched Cal's face remain impassive, but there was a little flash of something at the end. And he turned to Landon apologetically. "Let's just open the door."

Landon said nothing. And he didn't move. It wasn't so off-base. Her argument was good. But he didn't trust…anything. So why not let Cal lead, just like old times?

He said nothing to Hazeleigh, didn't even look at her, just opened the door. She lifted her chin and sailed into the outbuilding Henry had converted into a little detached bedroom and office.

They all filed in behind her. Jake and Zara, Henry, Cal. Landon hesitated. He thought about leaving. Just… leaving. Completely. Maybe he'd go back to Mississippi. Maybe he'd just start hiking to Alaska. Maybe…

But Hazeleigh's voice was strong and demanding as she faced the man who'd attacked her.

"Why did you try to kidnap me?"

Landon had to…see this through. He just had to. He turned in time to see the would-be kidnapper shrug his shoulders, looking totally unconcerned that he was tied up and being questioned by eight strangers. That didn't sit right. It *wasn't* right.

"Who sent you here?"

"We already asked that one," Henry muttered.

"A little birdie," the man said, then chuckled at his own joke.

"Where's my computer?"

The man smiled slyly. "What computer?"

She whipped her head around to look at him and his brothers. "Where's my computer?"

"He didn't have it when I tackled him," Jake said. "But I didn't know I was looking for a computer."

"We need it," Hazeleigh said firmly.

"Once it's daylight—"

"No, we need it now," she said, cutting off Cal. She gave the tied-up man one last haughty look. "You said you know me, but I don't know you."

"Oh, you know me."

Hazeleigh was clearly frustrated by that—clearly did not know the man—but she didn't argue. She looked at Zara, who nodded almost imperceptibly, and then they both left the building.

Landon followed. "That was it? Those were the oh-so-important questions we couldn't ask for you?"

She ignored him and looked at Zara. "You recognized him?"

"I think. He looks a lot different, but I'm pretty sure that's Hamilton Chinelly."

Hazeleigh frowned. "Who?"

"Don't you remember? He was one of Dad's ranch hands when Mom was sick."

"That was almost twenty years ago. Chinelly... Chinelly…" Hazeleigh was tapping her fingers together and Landon was about ready to come unwound, but Jake had a hand on his shoulder…like Cal had done before. Keeping him steady.

"Let them work it out," Jake said quietly.

Zara paced. Hazeleigh tapped. Landon wanted to howl in protest.

"Don't they have a connection to the Petersons?" Hazeleigh asked, pointing dramatically at Zara.

Zara stopped pacing. "Why's that matter?"

"Just…what was it? Do you remember?"

"I think a Chinelly married a Peterson. I remember thinking anyone related to Ham getting married was quite the accomplishment. He's never been the brightest or nicest man."

"Okay, town gossip. Blah, blah, blah. What does it *mean*?" Landon demanded.

"I think it means we need to go search the Peterson place. But first, I need my computer." And then she just took off. She strode across the yard, away from the glow of the porch light and toward the cabin where she'd nearly been kidnapped.

Landon made a strangled noise, but Jake's hand on his shoulder kept him from moving. But then Zara was there.

"Let him go," Zara said to Jake quietly. "They need to work some things out, and I need to talk to you."

Landon barely heard what Jake said in return, just felt the hand on his shoulder loosen, then he took off after Hazeleigh's quickly retreating form.

Was she insane? Was *everyone* insane? She could

hardly just go off on her own. "Where are you going?" he demanded once he was close enough not to yell.

Once he was calm enough to trust himself not to rage.

The sun was beginning to rise. They'd barely slept in something like two days. This was all spiraling out of his control.

"I am going to find my computer. My computer has the answers." She stopped briefly in the backyard of her cabin, searching the grass with the toe of her foot. Then she set out again. Off in the direction the kidnapper had run.

"Do you want to get caught? The cops? More kidnappers? They're all out there ready to take *you*, Hazeleigh."

She whirled to face him and flung her hands wide. "I want to live my damn life." The pink pearly light of dawn glinted so she appeared showered in something like gold. Fire. Everything. She'd been *everything* ever since she'd first smiled at him—that thunderclap. "For once I am going to do everything I can to make that happen instead of stand around waiting for someone else to make things right for me."

He wanted that for her. He wanted *everything* for her. To make it right, to help her make it right. Anything. Whatever it took. These emotions all whirled inside of him, with the exhaustion, with the failure, with the fear, and with this much bigger thing he didn't know what to do with. He'd never known what to do with.

She looked at him like all those emotions had shown up on his face. She even stepped toward him. "What's wrong?" she asked, like she cared. Like it mattered.

She reached up and touched his cheek. "Landon. What on earth is the matter?"

"I love you."

He'd never said those words. Not once.

Because no one, not once, had ever said them to him.

Chapter Eighteen

It might have been comical. Maybe it should have been. Landon had just said the three sweetest words he could possibly utter, and then looked so horrified by them, it was hard to be warmed.

But he had said them. And Hazeleigh didn't think it was a lie. What would be the point of a lie? He wasn't trying to get her to do something or believe something. He wasn't using love as a weapon. It was more like love had overwhelmed him and he didn't have the foggiest idea what to do with it.

She wanted to step closer, lean into him, but he seemed so frozen in shock by what he'd said, she held herself as still as he was holding himself.

"Is that the matter?" she asked quietly.

"I can't help you if I'm…compromised."

His eyes looked so anguished. She stroked his cheek. "Compromised. Now, you're being silly. You're exhausted."

"I knew something was wrong and I left you to the wolves!" he exploded. But he didn't move away, didn't pull away from her hand on his stubbled cheek.

She took that to heart. And she understood the

meaning beneath the words. "Landon, I know that guilt. I live that guilt. I felt something wrong myself going in there, but I talked myself out of it. Do you know how many times I've fought my gut, for worse or for better? Do you know how long I spent listening to my father tell me if those feelings I had were worth anything, I could have stopped Amberleigh from running away? How awful I've felt wondering why I couldn't have had a bad feeling that would have saved her from being murdered?"

He started to say her name, but she shook her head. "I know what guilt is, Landon, and it's misplaced here. You told me not to blame myself for everything that happens, so you can't blame yourself for not listening to your gut. We both ignored our feelings because feelings *aren't* facts. They're right sometimes, wrong other times. You can only do your best in the moment, and in the moment…we're both alive and well."

His hand closed over her wrist. "I could not live with myself if something happened to you. I cannot bear the thought of…" He licked his lips, clearly trying to clarify his thoughts before he spoke. "You can't be alone. You need to take one of my brothers and—"

"One of your brothers? Why on earth would I do that?"

"They have the necessary emotional distance. Nothing will cloud their decision-making. It's better, safer—"

"I don't care about the necessary emotional distance. I care about *you*, Landon…" Did she love him? The words had bubbled up, unbidden, in response, but maybe that was just a reflex. She'd convinced herself she was in love before.

This was more—deeper…stronger. She just *felt* it. And she couldn't explain it exactly or rationalize her way through it.

It simply was.

That was the difference, wasn't it? That it just was. That it felt right, without any need for convincing or reasons. He was good, and he cared. He kissed her and the world fell away. He wanted her to be safe, without a worry for himself.

She trusted him. And now she needed to trust herself.

"I love you, too."

He inhaled sharply. "Don't…say that."

"Why wouldn't I say that? I mean it."

"But—"

"No *buts*. You won't argue my feelings, Landon. I won't listen to it. Not anymore." Too many people had tried to tell her what to feel or what she should be, and she'd listened for far too long. That would be over now.

Landon swallowed. "No one's ever said that to me."

"No one? Surely your mother…" But she trailed off at his bleak expression. No one had ever… Her heart broke. She'd had a rough relationship with her father, but her mother had been love itself. Her sisters, for all their arguments and complications, had always expressed love to each other.

To grow up without that. She put her other hand on his other cheek, rose to her toes and pressed her mouth to his. "Well, now I have, and you'll have to get used to hearing it."

"Hazeleigh…" He sounded so strangled. "There are things you don't know about me."

"I'm sure there are things you don't know about me. Does that change anything for you?"

"Of course not, but—"

"Then it doesn't change anything for me. I don't believe love is some magical, easy feeling and we'll skip happily into the sunset, Landon. I don't say 'I love you' because I think everything's *fine* now. Maybe we find something about each other we can't get over. Maybe we don't."

"Doesn't this right here just prove my point? The sun is rising and we're standing in broad daylight arguing about *love*. We need to be focused on the man who tried to kidnap you."

"Yes, I suppose that's a good focus."

"You suppose," he scoffed. "You can't be out here in broad daylight. You don't know when the cops might come. You don't know who else is out there. Whoever this Hamilton Chinelly is working for. They're all out there and you're a target to them all."

"Maybe," she replied. Something about his lack of calm had her feeling the opposite. The panic had been in the not knowing of it all, but now they had clues. There were steps to follow.

"Hazeleigh."

He sounded so…broken. She wished she could ease that brokenness in him, but if love couldn't, then nothing could at the moment. So she'd go for the facts. "There's something bigger here. I'm a pawn, yes. A scapegoat. But doesn't this feel…" She trailed off. She couldn't put her finger on it. "The man—this Hamilton, who I don't really remember though I never enjoyed ranch work the way Zara did—waited in my cabin for me to appear. Waited. Then he botched the kidnapping attempt."

"He doesn't know anything," Landon said, finally sounding more like himself. "You could see it on his face. He *thought* he knew things, but the more I asked, the more confused he got."

"If you were trying to…hide something, or find something, would you send that guy to do your dirty work?"

"It's a distraction." Landon blinked, then focused on her. "Why would it be a distraction?"

"I don't know, but I don't want to be distracted." She squinted into the rising sun. "Maybe this all works in our favor. We're not on our own anymore. It's the nine of us against whoever is out there."

"Whoever is out there plus the cops."

She supposed that was true, and she had no desire to deal with the cops until she'd found more. But she felt… hopeful. She looked up at Landon. There were shadows underneath his eyes, lines dug around his mouth.

He loved her.

And she loved him.

"Why don't you help me find my computer? And then we'll both get some rest." She took his hand, because Zara had said it herself. Just because you were strong didn't mean you couldn't use support. "We're going to need it."

THEY DIDN'T FIND the computer, despite looking for an hour. They retraced the kidnapper's footsteps along with those of his brothers' who'd gone after Hamilton. No laptop.

Eventually Landon convinced Hazeleigh to go back to the ranch house. Of course, in order to convince her he had to agree to go himself. They'd both been awake too long. Too strung out on stress and…

Love.

She'd said she loved him.

It made everything weigh a little heavier, even as it lightened something inside of him that had been weighed down so long he'd stopped noticing it. He didn't know what to do with that—heavy and light, confusing and…right. Somehow.

"Either he hid the computer, or someone was waiting to take it," Landon said as they walked back to the ranch.

Hazeleigh held his hand and frowned. She had dark circles under her eyes, and her shoulders were slumped. Exhaustion clung to her like a physical entity. He let go of her hand and slid his arm around her shoulders. She leaned in as they walked.

"Why hide it? Did he think he'd get back to it? What does he think he can get off of it without me?"

"The way you explained it he only let you go because we came. So maybe he thought he'd come back and get you at another time."

She chewed on her lip. "Maybe. Can't say as I like *that* thought."

"Yeah, me neither." He held her a little closer. "But I still don't know what they thought they'd find on your computer."

Hazeleigh sighed as they reached the house. She paused, looking up at the house with a frown. "Landon,

I didn't want to involve anyone in this and now everyone's involved."

He didn't know what to say to that because everyone was involved. There was no going back now. He could maybe secret her away somewhere again, but it would have to be farther and—

"I think I'm actually...relieved," she said, interrupting his thoughts on how to fix things for her. "It feels more like... It's just..." She looked up at him, studying his face, as if she didn't know what she was looking for. "I know Zara's my only real family here, but she's marrying Jake. And he's a Thompson brother. And then Kate has been one of my friends since forever, and she's involved with one of your brothers and maybe this is what... Well, maybe it's what family is like when your own wasn't very much to speak of. One you cobble together yourself."

Family. Cal had mentioned that, too. He'd always assumed it would just be the six of them. They were all so alone, so...well, screwed up, he hadn't pictured picket fences and Wyoming ranches and marriages.

But it was nice. It was *good*.

"Maybe it is," he agreed.

"Family should stick together. They should help each other." She kept looking at him, like she was waiting for him to have some kind of answer.

"I...guess." He didn't really know what family *should* do. He only knew he had his brothers' backs and they had his.

"So it's good. We'll work together, figure this out and we won't let anyone get in trouble because of me."

"It isn't because of *you*, Hazeleigh. You didn't ask to be framed for your boss's murder."

"Okay, but…"

"No *buts*. We're not being martyrs, remember?"

She wrinkled her nose. "I guess. Hard habit to break."

"That it is," he agreed.

Then she smiled up at him. "I guess we can learn to break it together."

He tucked a strand of hair behind her ear, enjoying the feel of her skin under his fingertips. She was safe, and now there were eight of them to keep her safe. She wouldn't like it phrased like that, so he didn't say it out loud. But it settled him nonetheless.

Everything would be okay. They'd fight like hell to make it okay.

He lowered his mouth to hers, half convinced all that love talk in her backyard had been a sleepless delusion, but she leaned into him, kissing him back, and he knew… Whatever they'd found here, just the two of them, it wasn't going anywhere.

Someone was clearing their throat. Landon struggled to come up for air, and when he did Zara was standing on the porch. Scowling.

"Why don't you just *call* the cops and ask them to come arrest you?" Zara said irritably. "Standing in the front yard making out, for heaven's sake."

Hazeleigh smiled a little and disentangled herself from him. But she still held his hand as they walked into the house, and that felt like…something. Family cobbled together. Love and connection.

Zara led them to the basement, where she'd set up cots. If the cops came, Hazeleigh would be out of sight and Landon could help take her somewhere if they got another warrant to search the house—always a possibility.

Zara gave Landon a disapproving look, but left them alone in the basement without saying anything.

Then finally, they had a chance to sleep. Landon thought he should say something—about love or families or keeping her safe—but she was asleep the minute she was horizontal. So he crawled into his own cot and did the same.

When he woke up, she was gone.

Panic blinded him, and he couldn't think past it. He jumped out of his cot and rushed upstairs, only to find her sitting at the kitchen table, a plate of crumbs at her elbow and Kate standing in the kitchen area eyeing him suspiciously.

"You're up," Hazeleigh said casually. "Kate set me up with her computer from the fort. It doesn't have access to Mr. Field's emails like mine did, but it does let me see some things he saved to the historical server, including the photograph that was missing from that album."

"How long did you sleep?" he demanded, ignoring Kate's considering gaze.

She turned to him and smiled. "I woke up just about fifteen minutes ago, so not much longer than you. It's hard to sleep when all this is going on."

"Sit," Kate instructed him. "Eat."

He obeyed, if only because he didn't have the foggiest idea what else to do.

Hazeleigh turned the computer monitor toward him.

"Here," she said, pointing to a picture on the screen. "This is the picture whoever killed Mr. Field took."

Landon frowned at the screen, squinting. "It just looks like an old shack."

"It is an old shack." She pointed to the corner of the picture where there was the fuzzy edge of another building. "But this is the corner of the schoolhouse— I'm almost certain."

"There weren't any other buildings out there around the schoolhouse."

"No, this is a picture from 1897. The shack either fell down or was torn down long before the schoolhouse was abandoned, but what if there was some kind of cellar or something? In the ground?"

"You don't honestly think the mythical gold is in some hole in the ground on Peterson land?" Kate said, sliding a plate next to Landon.

He murmured his thanks and they all peered at the screen.

"It doesn't have to be there," Hazeleigh said. "Someone only has to think it is."

The side door opened. Zara, Jake and Cal entered, probably after having done ranch work all afternoon.

"You should have slept longer," Zara chided.

"Slept as long as I could," Hazeleigh replied with a smile. "Where's everyone else?"

"They're coming," Cal said. "They were taking care of our friend Hamilton."

"Taking care?"

"Just drove him out a way. Dropped him off in the middle of nowhere with some supplies so he won't die.

But far enough away he can't be a problem until we've solved our own."

Landon supposed it was the best option, though he would have liked to have left him in the middle of nowhere with *no* supplies and left him to rot.

Dunne, Henry and Brody returned not long after, saying they'd been successful. If Hamilton went to the cops, it'd be his word against theirs, and he'd have to explain why he was at the ranch in the first place, so it wasn't likely he'd go after them.

They positioned themselves around the table after getting snacks and drinks, settling in to see what was next.

It was exactly what Hazeleigh had said. A family. Cobbled together between a lot of people who hadn't been blessed with the best genetic relatives.

Landon took Hazeleigh's hand under the table and she smiled at him. But then she released it and stood. "Now that everyone's here, I have the beginnings of a plan."

"You do?" he and Zara said at the same time.

"I do," she said firmly. "I think we need to search the Peterson land. Something is going on there or centered there. The little girl I saw? She mentioned her mother. I don't know how a little girl could connect, but it points to the fact there are people there, one way or another."

She looked so…in charge. So sure of herself. It made him oddly proud.

"It's a big spread," Zara said, but she was clearly considering it. "Lots of buildings. All in bad condition."

"Which means there's a lot of places for people to hide, undetected," Cal said. "If a killer is really hiding out there, it's a dangerous proposition. One maybe better left for the—"

"Don't say police, Cal. You know that isn't true," Henry muttered irritably.

"They're law enforcement."

"And we're trained, better than small county law enforcement, to deal with an enemy hiding in a broad, unknown terrain," Jake returned.

"Trained?" Hazeleigh said, and Landon didn't have to look at her to know she was staring at *him* in confusion.

Everyone around them got a little still, a *lot* uncomfortable. Jake cleared his throat. "Sorry, I thought Zara would have said."

"I can keep a secret," Zara muttered, but she gave Landon an accusatory look, as if it was *his* fault Hazeleigh didn't know.

"I'm sorry. There's some kind of…secret?" Hazeleigh asked, in that careful, prim voice she only used when she was hurt.

Landon sighed and stared at his hands. Here it was. He'd been fooling himself to think anything could be different. "I was in the military. We were…all in the military."

"Oh."

"I told you there were things you didn't know about me."

"So you did." She blew out a breath. "I wish I'd known. Then I might not have been so insistent on running away. But, now that I do, I agree with Jake. You all are far more equipped to help."

"Help? Uh, no." Landon shook his head. "We'll handle it."

"No," Hazeleigh returned evenly, holding his gaze. "Zara and I are going, too."

Chapter Nineteen

Hazeleigh didn't quite know how to feel about this military thing. Not so much that Landon had been in the military and hadn't told her, but that it was supposed to be some kind of secret. That seemed odd and strange. Why would it be a secret?

But she couldn't deal with that right now. There was a murderer to find. "It's a big spread, like Zara said. Zara and I have a much better idea of the lay of the land than you six do."

"We also know what to do when someone shoots at us."

She raised an eyebrow at Landon. "Get shot in the arm?" she replied sweetly.

"Better than the head," Henry replied with his usual lack of tact. Because she could clearly see poor Mr. Field's body, with exactly that. A shot to the head.

She stiffened and Landon's hand came over hers. She had a feeling he was about to stand up and defend her, but that wasn't necessary. She opened her mouth to keep speaking, but Henry spoke first.

"Sorry," Henry grumbled.

It felt a bit like a coup to earn an apology from him

without any prompting. She'd take it as a good sign. She forced herself to smile even though she figured she'd probably gone a little pale there.

"If you all want to draw up some kind of military plan, that's fine. Maybe even smart. But you need someone—or in this case some*ones*—who know the land. Where the buildings are. What to look for."

Jake shook his head. "I don't like it."

"No one asked you to like it," Zara replied. "It's the smart thing to do. Isn't it, Cal?"

All eyes turned to Cal, and for the first time since she'd known him, Hazeleigh thought he looked a little uncomfortable.

"In your unbiased, military opinion," Zara continued. "Do we go, or do we stay?"

Cal sighed. "Since I know Zara knows how to handle a rifle, I'd say she could go." He frowned at Hazeleigh. "Can you handle a gun?"

Hazeleigh had always hated guns, but Dad had insisted she know how to use one. "I don't like to, but I can."

"Cal's not in charge," Jake said stubbornly.

"No. I am," Hazeleigh said. "And I say we go."

"That'a girl," Zara said. She turned to Jake. "Look, we'll play it your way. Draw up your tactical plans. We'll follow them. But we go. You need us."

"And then what?" Cal asked. "Let's say we find the murderer, maybe even proof. What then?"

"Then we call the cops."

"And if they don't listen?" Henry asked.

"Thomas will," Zara said loyally.

"He's your cousin. The cops might not listen to *him*, even if he's one of them," Dunne pointed out.

"He'll find a way," Jake said, not sounding all that happy about it. "He found a way to help when Zara was in trouble. And look, I don't think anyone *wants* to believe Hazeleigh did it. We just have to prove she didn't. Whatever way we can."

"Together," Hazeleigh said, feeling the truth of that deep in her bones. "If we work together, we'll be all right. And we'll figure out who killed Mr. Field. He didn't deserve to die, especially if it's about this silly bank robbery." She looked back down at the picture. Something about it…bothered her. "I want to look at this picture, in person. This picture means something to someone, and we need to get to the bottom of it."

"Landon, you haven't said anything," Cal pointed out.

Hazeleigh looked down at him—he was still sitting at the table with an unreadable expression. But slowly, he stood.

"Here's how it will go. I'll take Hazeleigh to the spot with the picture. The rest of you will fan out on the edges of the property in teams of two and slowly close the circle, doing a sweep. We'll take walkies. Keep in constant contact. If one group comes into contact with someone, we try to avoid it. If we find evidence of people, we investigate. We'll go at night."

"Tonight," Hazeleigh said. "The longer this goes on, the more chance whatever is going on just disappears." Especially if they found the gold.

She'd never believed in this bank-robbery gold. It was too far-fetched. She'd spent years following Mr.

Field down every avenue of research and there'd never even been a glimmer of reality in all the stories passed down.

She still wasn't sure she believed the mythology, but what she *did* believe was that someone out there thought it was true. And was going to kill to find this supposed gold.

Something in that picture was a clue. She just didn't know what it was yet.

She looked around the kitchen—six cowboys, who'd apparently all been in the military, and her fearless sister. Along with her childhood friend, who'd hold down the fort, so to speak.

She never would have believed this for herself. Confidence. Bravery. A strong, sweet man who loved her. A family they'd made themselves out of a lot of happenstance.

Maybe unbelievable things could be true. Maybe there *was* old bank-robbery gold out there. She didn't dare say it. She knew how people rolled their eyes when Mr. Field had said it. It wasn't what was important anyway. What was important was finding out who'd killed Mr. Field. Who wanted her to take the fall for it.

"I don't want anyone to take chances for me—" Hazeleigh began.

"Oh, stuff it," Zara said firmly. "Family takes chances for each other. And *this* family takes chances to do what's right. Everyone got it?"

Everyone agreed, in words or nods. Everyone.

Except Landon.

LANDON HAD OUTLINED the plan to everyone. He'd listened as his brothers argued details, pros and cons, what weapons to use, what time to leave. They honed the plan with what little time they had.

Landon didn't know what he was feeling. It was different from a military mission, because Hazeleigh was involved. Because *lives* were involved—not just the idea of being alive, but actually leaving something behind.

Perhaps it was the first time in his life he didn't feel particularly fatalistic about an outcome. He wanted everyone—including himself—to make it. To the other side, not the next mission.

There was no room for all that want, that worry, that fear. There was only moving forward with the plan.

At nightfall, they all assembled, going over the plan one last time.

Dunne and Cal were going to be in the truck, just in case. Zara and Jake were a pair, Landon and Hazeleigh, then Henry and Brody, all on horseback.

Flashlight in hand, Cal pointed at a map Landon had printed out and went over the plan one last time. "We spread out. Wait for the signal before we all start pulling in. Except for Hazeleigh and Landon, who will go straight for the schoolhouse. Any sign of *anything*, you walkie and everyone stops. We do this together or not at all."

Landon looked down at Hazeleigh in the quickly fading light. She was the only one who didn't nod or look to be in agreement, but she didn't say anything. Dunne and Cal went for the truck, and everyone else got on their horses. Jake and Zara had the farthest to go to get to their checkpoint, so they set off first, Henry and Brody not far behind.

Hazeleigh was hesitating, but eventually she got up in her saddle, so he did, too.

"You'll let me know if you get one of those bad feelings, huh?"

She looked over at him and smiled. "Only if you promise to do the same."

He could tell she was nervous, simply by the way she held Buttercup's reins.

"I'm not going to let anything happen to you," he said. A promise. A vow.

"What about yourself?"

"Hazeleigh."

"No, I know… I just keep thinking about how Jake took that bullet meant for Cal last year. That's what family does, I suppose. That's what love does. And I guess I ran because…well, mostly because of panic, but a lot because I didn't want anyone taking any bullets for me."

They both urged their horses into a trot as they made their way back toward the schoolhouse.

"But in the last…day, I guess, I started to think maybe that's because I didn't think I was *worth* it. That's sort of been the thing I had to pull myself out of since last year. That I might be worth something."

Landon wanted to assure her she was worth *everything*, but his throat was closed tight. Because he'd been there. The only thing that had given him any worth had been the military, Team Breaker, and he supposed that, in the worst of circumstances, he and his brothers had banded together. *Together.*

So he said nothing at all, and Hazeleigh continued.

"I don't want anyone to be hurt because of me. I

don't. But I would want to stop someone else from getting hurt. I'd want to step in front of that bullet like Jake did. Because that's love. I want to give that to other people—so I guess that means I might need to let other people give it to me."

She looked over at him, though he couldn't see her face in the darkening night. Just the impression of her head moving toward him.

"So maybe you're not about to let anything happen to me, but the same goes. I think it goes across the board. Because this isn't just about you rushing in to save the day. It's us all working together to right a wrong."

Which was everything he'd been through with his brothers. For years now. But they'd begun to let other people in. Let love in. And it made everything more… dangerous. Heavy and scary and stressful.

But a real life, with a richness that the military, and righting wrongs, hadn't given them. A future to look forward to—to build toward.

"Then let's right this one."

Chapter Twenty

Once they reached the schoolhouse, the time for intro-
spection and thoughts on love and family were gone.
Hazeleigh had to figure out what was going on. She
had to get to the bottom of things. If nothing else so
she could have her *life* back. A better life than she'd
been living for a long time.

Something in that picture showing the space between the schoolhouse and the old shed that no longer
existed had to give them some clue. Some next step.

Someone had to be here. Someone had to be on this
property. Maybe it all connected. Maybe it didn't.

But they'd find the answers. They had to.

Darkness had engulfed everything, and if there were
people on the Peterson property, they were very well
hidden. Hazeleigh didn't let that depress her. For now,
her focus was on the picture and the reality.

Every so often Landon pulled out a flashlight to
make sure they were on the right track. When they got
to the schoolhouse, he helped her off her horse, clearly
reluctant to turn on the light.

"We're awfully exposed," he said, sounding uncertain and not letting go of her waist even now that she was steady on the ground.

"No bad feelings yet."

He huffed out a laugh. "Yeah, that makes me feel better after all our talk about feelings not mattering as much as we think." But he released her, and the very narrow beam of a light flipped on.

She made out the schoolhouse and the patch of grass around them. She pulled out her phone and brought up the picture that she'd saved on it.

She oriented herself and then tried to find what would have been the remains of the shack. Landon followed behind her, keeping the flashlight pointed on the ground in front of Hazeleigh.

They worked as a team, without even having to discuss it. She knew without looking that he was on high alert for anyone around them, and it allowed her to focus. She looked from the picture to the ground, walked in circles. "A few spots have been…" She poked her toe against the odd unearthed bumps. "It's like someone's been digging out here."

"Looking for the gold?"

"I suppose, though they tried to cover their tracks by putting the dirt back." Hazeleigh looked on her phone at the picture—it was over one hundred years old. Obviously things had changed, and the land had been worked at least a while after this had been taken. Whenever the shed had been removed or fallen down, surely whatever had been hidden in it would have been found then. "Why doesn't this add up?"

"There's something we're missing," Landon agreed.

"Maybe we're looking at all the pieces too closely. Too…separately."

"Maybe, but I don't know what else…" Hazeleigh trailed off. There was something different about the picture besides the shed. The corner of the schoolhouse was…brick. Not the wood it should have been. "Point your light at the schoolhouse."

Landon did as he was told. The narrow beam illuminated the schoolhouse corner enough to see the wood was old and worn and splintering. Why would anyone have covered up brick with wood? Particularly a schoolhouse that hadn't been in use in some time. When had it happened? Why had it happened?

Did it mean anything or was she driving herself insane?

She moved for the corner, Landon right behind her shining the light at the building. "This is different than the picture," she explained. "In the picture it's brick. But here it's wood." She trailed her fingers along the wood, following Landon's beam of light.

"Someone's already been here," Landon said flatly. "Look." He pointed the beam of light at the other side of the corner, where the wood had been ripped away. "I don't think it was like that before."

"No, it wasn't." Hazeleigh was struck completely dumb for a moment. "Was Mr. Field right? Was there really bank gold here?"

"Something was here." Landon flashed the light into the hole in the wood. "Something was hidden between the wood and the brick."

"But if they sent someone to kidnap me, aren't they

still looking for something? They had the picture since the murder, and this just happened."

"So the picture didn't give them the information they needed. But something had to have."

"My computer." It only dawned on her because Landon had all that crazy computer equipment that could do who knew what. "My computer would have had a map of pictures connecting to the land. I'm not sure how they would have logged on and found it, but I did have a document on there placing the pictures on the map." Hazeleigh blew out a breath, because the puzzle just kept getting more confusing. "But you guys stopped Hamilton. We didn't find my computer, but…"

"Maybe Hamilton handed off your computer, or hid it somewhere for someone else to find. Then allowed himself to be caught as a distraction."

"A distraction from *what*?" Irritation simmered through her. All these questions. No real answers. Worst of all… "If there was really gold from some old bank robbery, why would anyone need to go through all this trouble to kill? Why not just find it and go from there?"

"People will do a lot of things for money. I assume old, mythical gold might be worth a pretty penny."

"It still doesn't add up."

"No, it doesn't. Maybe we should join the search crew. See who we can round up out here. If nothing else, we know that little girl has a mother around here somewhere."

Hazeleigh knew he was probably right. There were no answers to be found here. No gold, either. Or maybe the gold had been found and was long gone now. But then wouldn't they leave? The girl? Whoever was involved? And why keep Hazeleigh's computer? Why distract with Hamilton Chinelly?

"Sometimes you just have to keep gathering clues until they start adding up," Landon said, placing a hand on her back and giving her a little pat. "We don't know whether they found something here or not, but we know they looked. That's...something."

Hazeleigh wanted to pout. It didn't feel like something. It felt like a whole lot of *nothing*. And nothing was starting to feel worse than danger or kidnapping attempts because *nothing* was starting to feel like it might be *forever* that the police thought she'd killed Mr. Field.

She leaned forward to look a little deeper into the space between the wood and the brick, but Landon clicked off his light. "Hazeleigh, don't move. Not an inch. Not an inch, okay?"

"Bu—"

She didn't even get the word out before Landon jumped forward and knocked her to the ground.

THE EXPLOSION SOUNDED, a terrifying *boom*, and heat engulfed his entire body. He covered Hazeleigh in every way he could. Something rained down on them. Shrapnel? An old memory tried to take over, but he pushed it away.

Not war. Just Wyoming. The objects raining down on them didn't exactly hurt. Because they were just clumps of dirt. Whatever had caused the explosion had been underground. In the holes. Someone hadn't been digging up supposed gold, they'd been setting explosives.

Landon's ears rang, his skin burned, but he could feel Hazeleigh's scrambled heartbeat beneath him and the heavy rise and fall of her breathing. Okay. She was okay.

But someone wanted them dead.

Them...or someone else? If Hamilton was a distraction, how would anyone predict they'd come here?

When a problem was more complicated than an answer, maybe that was the answer in and of itself. His problem wasn't their problem.

Maybe the problem, the confusion, came because they were in the *middle* of something.

But he couldn't think that thought through. They had to get out of here in case there were more explosives. Landon blinked open his eyes, tried to survey the damage. Smoke burned in his lungs, and the schoolhouse was on fire. Enough fire to see by.

"Are you okay?" Hazeleigh asked, her voice a rasp beneath him. "Landon, are you all right?"

"I'm fine. I'm okay." He probably had some burns, but nothing too bad. She'd likely have some bruises from him knocking her to the ground, so maybe it evened out. "Don't move just yet, okay?"

He surveyed the night around them. The explosion had to have been loud enough to be heard for miles around, which meant his brothers would be worried about them. He shifted ever so carefully so he could pull his walkie out of his pocket.

"All good here. Stay where you are for now."

There was the quiet chorus of affirmatives in response. There could be more explosives out there, so they had to be careful. Especially with the horses. They didn't appear to be serious bombs, causing a significant amount of damage, but they'd definitely ripped up the ground they'd been buried in.

Why? Why? Why?

He had to trust the answers would come, because right now he had to get Hazeleigh away from potential danger. They'd figured out the reasoning for the photograph, sort of, and now they knew someone was out there.

Maybe a retreat was in order.

"When I get up, you're going to run for Buttercup. Get on her and go." His mind scrambled for the best, safest place for her to go. "Toward where Cal and Dunne are in the truck. Walkie them so they can meet you."

"Landon, what about you?"

He opened his mouth to say he'd be right behind, but...

Someone was coming or watching. He could feel it. He knew it the way he'd known to dive and cover her. A tenseness in the air. A quiet ticking of something he'd honed in the military. His gut told him something was coming, and he wanted Hazeleigh far away from it.

"I'll be behind you."

"Landon, we should stick together."

"We will. But first, I need you to get to Cal and Dunne. Okay? When I say to, get up and run and don't stop. Get on Buttercup and don't stop. Walkie as you ride. I will be right behind you, on your six. I promise." He wouldn't stay here to fight off whatever was coming, but he'd protect her, no matter what it took.

She let out a shuddery breath. "If you break that promise, I'm going to be really mad."

"Understood. Now, I'm going to count to three. Pop up. You run. Do not worry about me. I will be behind you. There might be some distance, but I *will* be behind you."

"All right. All right."

Landon gave them both a moment to breathe, to ready themselves. Then he began the countdown quietly in her ear. *"Go!"*

She popped up in time with him and took off running for Buttercup. Landon pulled his gun out of its holster and followed her slowly, watching the world around them. When Hazeleigh stopped at Buttercup and didn't get on, he had to tamp down his impatience to speak quietly.

"Go, Hazeleigh," he said as quietly as he could over the crackling blaze around them so she could hear.

"I can't." Hazeleigh angled her body slightly, and in the flickering flames he made out a little girl. It must be the little girl Hazeleigh had talked to the other day. Obviously they couldn't leave her behind. They'd have to take her with them.

But as Landon moved forward, he realized why Hazeleigh had said she couldn't move.

The little girl's face was streaked with dirt or grease or smoke. Her hair was half falling out of a band. She wore dirty jeans and an even dirtier sweatshirt. Her eyes were flat as she stared right at him.

In each hand, she held a very large gun—one was pointed at Hazeleigh.

And now, one was pointed at him.

Chapter Twenty-One

"Drop the gun," the little girl said. Her voice, high-pitched and lilting, sounded like she belonged on a children's show. But Hazeleigh had no doubt she was serious. She had her fingers wrapped around the triggers. "The walkies, too."

Hazeleigh didn't know whether to be more terrified that the girl was a good shot and knew what she was doing, or that she might accidentally shoot them.

Hazeleigh glanced back at Landon. He looked positively thunderstruck. Though he held his gun, he didn't aim it at the girl. It was pointed at the ground, even though she had two guns fixed on them.

This was not good.

"Do I need to count to three?" the little girl asked, and there was no hesitation, no quiver in her voice. She was in control and knew just what she was after.

Landon looked at Hazeleigh, and she…didn't know what to do. He could hardly shoot a little girl…even if the girl was armed. She gave him a slight nod and he nodded back. He crouched to the ground and placed his gun on the overturned earth.

"The walkies," the girl said, gesturing with both guns.

The move made Hazeleigh nervous enough to fumble with hers. It clattered to the ground while Landon calmly placed his next to his gun.

"Did you plant those explosives yourself?" he asked, taking a careful step toward Hazeleigh.

"Don't come closer," the girl said.

Landon held up his hands a little, like a gesture of surrender. The poor schoolhouse crackled and creaked as the fire licked up the boards.

"Now, I don't know what's going on or who you are, but my brothers are on their way. I don't want you to get hurt, sweetheart, so why don't you put the guns down and—"

The little girl snorted and even Hazeleigh sighed. The Southern drawl could be charming, but what little girl holding guns aimed at adults wanted to be called *sweetheart*?

"Doubt it. I heard you telling them to stand down on your walkie. Besides, they probably didn't get far. No one gets far here."

Those words sent a cold chill up Hazeleigh's spine, but she tried not to let it show. The girl wasn't paying attention to her, even though one gun was pointed in her direction. She'd correctly guessed Landon was the bigger threat and focused more on him.

But... "I helped you," Hazeleigh said softly. "I let you have that flashlight and my gloves."

There was the flicker of something in the little girl's expression, but she didn't drop the guns. "I don't know you," she said with a jerk of her shoulders. "I stole those things fair and square. You didn't *let* me have them."

But she had. She'd tried to give them back. She

hadn't been threatening or cold. She'd been skittish, and alone, but not…angry.

"Where's your mother?" Hazeleigh asked gently.

The little girl's mouth firmed, and she adjusted the guns, like they were getting too heavy. But she wasn't about to drop them, that was for sure.

"If I bring you to him, he'll let her go. So you have to come with me."

"Who's him?" Landon asked, clearly trying to match Hazeleigh's quiet, calm tone. Not entreating, not condescending. Just like they were having a normal conversation.

With no guns pointed at anyone.

The girl said nothing, and that quiet refusal to answer made the chill in Hazeleigh's spine spread to her gut.

"We'll go. Won't we, Landon?" she said, not looking at Landon. She kept her gaze on the little girl. On the guns.

Landon hesitated. Hazeleigh knew he wanted to press more, ask more questions and demand some answers.

But he didn't. "Sure, we'll go. I guess you'll lead the way?"

Again, something flickered in her expression, but Hazeleigh didn't know what it was this time. Uncertainty of some kind.

"What's your name?"

"None of your business," the little girl muttered. She frowned at both of them. "You," she said, pointing to Landon. "Take five steps—no less, no more."

Landon nodded, his hands still slightly up in the

surrender position. Then he took five careful steps—
long strides—that put him almost next to Hazeleigh.
He began to take another one.

"I said five," the girl snapped, positioning both guns
to aim at him.

Without thinking it through, Hazeleigh stepped in
front of him. Gently, Landon moved her aside. He was
calm and collected.

"I miscounted," he said, attempting a smile at the
girl.

She didn't smile or soften in return. "I didn't."

They all stood there, Landon next to her, the girl
with the guns in front of them still pointed, while the
fire crackled.

She said nothing. They said nothing.

Hazeleigh had the strangest urge to start *laughing*.

"Okay," Landon said gently, whether at his wit's end
or sensing Hazeleigh was at hers. "You're trying to figure out a way to get us to go where you want without
one of us overpowering you."

"You try to overpower me, I shoot you."

"I don't think you want to shoot us," Landon replied
gently. Then he considered the look on her face in the
firelight. "Or at least not Hazeleigh."

"Thought your name was Zara."

"Zara is my twin sister." ·

"So you're a liar. I don't care about shooting liars."

Hazeleigh swallowed. She agreed with Landon—the
little girl didn't *want* to shoot anyone. But that didn't
mean she wouldn't. There was a desperation in her that
made Hazeleigh very nervous. Still, she smiled as best

she could while the schoolhouse burned down. "Won't you tell me your name?"

"Bigfoot," the little girl replied.

"All right, Bigfoot," Landon replied easily enough. "How about this. You tell us where you want us to go. We'll go, you follow, guns pointed. That'll work, won't it?"

"Like I'm gonna take *your* advice when *you're* my prisoner," she scoffed, sounding every inch a little girl.

Hazeleigh couldn't help but feel sorry for her. Something was very wrong if a ten-year-old was wandering around *alone* with two big guns trying to... Her mother. She was trying to get someone to let her mother go.

"We can help," Hazeleigh said. "We can help you, if you let us."

"Why would you help me?"

"Because it's the right thing to do," Landon said firmly. He took a step toward the girl, then another. "Go ahead and hand over the guns and you have my word that I'll help—"

One of the guns went off. On purpose, or by accident, Hazeleigh didn't have a clue, but it caused a loud, shocking slam of sound against the night around them.

Hazeleigh screamed in surprise, Landon hit the deck and the girl fell backward, probably from the harsh recoil of the gun that was far too big for her frame. Landon was back on his feet in seconds, clearly unhurt. Wherever she'd been shooting, she hadn't hit anybody, thank God.

Without thinking, Hazeleigh moved forward to help the little girl get up, but she scrambled back, angling the guns in Hazeleigh's direction again. "No. Don't come any closer. I'll shoot you. I will."

"I want to help."

"I don't care. Step back. Now."

Hazeleigh did as she was told. She looked over at Landon. He shrugged his shoulders, clearly as much at a loss as she was. The girl was dangerous, but neither of them were willing to hurt her to disarm her.

"If someone has your mother nearby, won't they be coming here to see what the commotion is?" Landon asked gently.

"They'll round up all your people first. I've got time. I've got time." She repeated it like she was convincing herself. "They aren't stupid. I have to do this my way. *My* way. I'm not going to fail."

Hazeleigh's heart just about broke. No matter how dangerous this girl was, she was trying so hard to save her mother. She clearly believed she was doing something right. She kept one gun pointed at them and looked wildly around, then her hand shot out and grabbed a bag that had been on the ground behind her. She pulled something out of it and threw it at Landon.

"Tie your hands together. And make it good. I really only need one of you. You make me mad, I'll hit you this time."

Landon sighed and looked at Hazeleigh. "I guess we'll have to do what she says," he said to her. Very seriously. And she realized what he was trying to tell her.

They'd go with the girl, because that was the only way to help her. Because he wanted to help this little girl who'd shot at him, just like Hazeleigh wanted to.

So Hazeleigh nodded and held out her hands.

LANDON KEPT ONE eye on the little girl while he carefully tied the wire around Hazeleigh's wrists. Then he tied what little was left of the wire around his own. He didn't tighten the knots and kept a little room in the bonds so there'd be an easy enough escape, but didn't make it too obvious that was what he was doing.

"It's not really long enough, and I can only do one of my hands."

"I could just shoot you and leave you here. I think they only want her."

"Trust me, they'll want me, too."

Whoever *they* were had clearly terrorized this little girl. He cared less about avoiding getting shot—been there, done that—and more about finding out who was behind this whole mess. Not just because they'd hurt Hazeleigh, but because they'd driven this little girl to… this.

He recognized that desperation, that hopeless panic. He'd seen it in his biological brothers' eyes. He'd never been able to stop them from ruining their own lives. He'd never been able to save them.

He was going to find a way to save this little girl.

"Here," Hazeleigh said softly. She tried to arrange her hands to help him tie off his second wrist. It was a struggle, and he could tell the little girl had grown impatient, but they did the best they could.

"She needs help," Hazeleigh whispered.

"I know. We'll give it to her. Let's just try to keep her talking."

"Shut up," the little girl said. She stalked over to them. She'd left one gun behind in the dark, but still held the other. It was far too big and powerful for her. Landon thought he could reach out and rip it from her hands.

As if she'd read his mind, she angled her body so her gun hand was out of his reach. She reached forward with her other hand and clipped a bright pink dog leash, of all things, to one of the loops around his and Hazeleigh's wrists.

She pulled. "Follow me," she said.

He shared a glance with Hazeleigh. They seemed to be on the same page. Worried about the girl, but well aware she was dangerous if they weren't careful with how they dealt with her. So they fell into step, wrists tied together so they had to do an awkward sideways shuffle step to keep up with the girl's purposeful strides into the night.

Landon looked at the leash. One clean jerk and he could overpower her. She'd likely drop the gun, though it wasn't a done deal, and it was clear she was volatile enough, desperate enough, to shoot them.

He kept his voice low, inclined his head as much toward Hazeleigh as he could. "Let's do our best to keep her talking. Calmly."

Hazeleigh nodded.

"Where do they have your mother?" he asked.

The little girl just grunted, gave the leash a tug that had them both stumbling a little. "You'll see."

"Why do they want me?" Hazeleigh asked.

She looked back at Hazeleigh. Now they were far enough away from the fire that it was impossible to make out her expression in the dark.

"You're the only one who knows."

"Knows what?"

"Everything the old man knew. My grandpa, I guess."

Grandpa. She had to mean Mr. Field.

"Who's your grandpa?" Hazeleigh asked, clearly confused.

Another hard tug, and this time Hazeleigh stumbled enough that it was only his quick thinking to redistribute their weight together that kept her from falling flat on her face.

"Doesn't matter," the girl said, and there was a hint of sadness in her detached, resigned acceptance. "All that matters is Mom."

"Can you tell me about your mom?" Landon asked.

"Stop talking!" the little girl shrieked, sounding as close to tears as she had this whole time.

Landon scrambled for a plan, but the little girl was... nothing he'd expected. All his normal reactions went out the window. He still needed to protect Hazeleigh, his brothers and her sister, who were out there somewhere along with this mysterious *they.*

But figuring out a way to stop this girl while still helping her felt like an impossible task.

So they walked in silence. Deeper and deeper into Peterson land. Based on the map in his head, he felt as though she was leading them to the very center of the property.

Where the old house was supposed to be.

The night drew darker around them, and it didn't take long for the fire to be completely out of sight behind swells of land and bunches of trees. The smell of smoke still hung in the air, but maybe no one would necessarily be able to see how to get to the mysterious fire.

Maybe. Far too many maybes.

"You know, we do really want to help you. This 'they' sounds pretty bad if they've got your mom. What can we do to help?"

"Nothing. No one can help us."

Landon felt that fatalism, deep in those old childhood hurts. "I know how that feels." His father's temper. The violence of it all. How it seemed so impossible to find someone to help. And then, as he'd gotten older, the failure of never being enough to help his brothers or his mother.

"You don't know anything."

"My dad liked to beat up on my brothers and me. It felt like a prison. When I was probably around your age, I thought I could escape. But I never could because no one would help me. I'd help you."

"I would, too," Hazeleigh said. "I gave you my flashlight, my gloves. I'd help."

"You're only saying that because I'm a little girl, but I can help myself." She grumbled something, then said very clearly, "You can only trust yourself."

"I used to believe that, too," Landon said softly. It wasn't comfortable, but he let those old emotions into his voice as he spoke. "I believed it for a very long time. And it never helped. Never got me out of anything bad. If anything, it sunk me deeper. Until I found people to trust and realized that…not everyone is out for themselves. There are good people out there. Who want to do right. Who want to help."

"Needing help or support doesn't make you weak," Hazeleigh added softly. "We want to—"

The little girl groaned in disgusted dissatisfaction.

"You two are the most annoying people in the entire world. You don't know me. You don't know anything about me. All you really want is for me to let you go." She gave a jerk and again Landon narrowly saved Hazeleigh from a tumble.

But she didn't keep walking and tugging them along. She stopped. A little beam of light clicked on. Landon could make out a tree and the shadow of the little girl.

She tied the leash around the tree. "I'll be back."

Landon didn't say anything, but he listened to the direction her footsteps went. In the distance, he could see the hint of a light.

With speed and ease, he loosened the knots on the wire around his wrists. It was time to do his best to save everyone.

Chapter Twenty-Two

Hazeleigh huffed out a breath. What *now*?

But after only a second of the little girl being gone, Landon's hands came to her shoulders.

"How did you get free?" she demanded.

"I want you to stay here," he said urgently, ignoring her question.

"Landon—"

"No, listen to me. I want to tell you to run, but I know you won't. You want to help her. I want to help her. But we still need answers, and we still need to stop whoever this is. So you'll stay here and if 'they' come and get you, at least I'll be around to save you. And her. And the mom. If we both disappear, I worry she'll get hurt. She wanted you more than me. If she comes back, you need to be here."

Hazeleigh's heart warmed. He wanted to help the little girl as much as she did. He was willing to risk *her*, and that was something. "So I stay here, and what will you do?"

"I'm going to see if I can find the others, or if the little girl was right and they've been rounded up. Then I'm going to see what's going on in that house."

"Okay."

"Hazeleigh…"

"No, it's okay. It's good."

"I don't want to leave you here."

"But you know you have to. It's okay. I'll be okay. They want me for something, so that means I'm not in any danger."

"That's hardly what that means," he said darkly. He sighed. "Hazeleigh, is it possible Mr. Field was this girl's grandpa? She said you're the only one who knows what the old man knew. Her grandpa."

"I know, but it doesn't make sense. He didn't have any kids as far as I know. Never married. Never with anyone. But as for possible?" Hazeleigh blew out a breath. "If that gold was real? Anything is possible."

"Yeah. Yeah." He gave her shoulders a squeeze. "Okay. Just…be careful. Okay?"

"Same goes." She hated the thought of separating, but it was the only way to try to protect themselves and the little girl.

He pressed a kiss to her mouth. "I'll be back. I promise."

"I love you."

There was a pause, and she knew he was absorbing those words no one else had ever given him. "I love you, too." And then he was gone.

She was in the dark alone, tied to a tree. It wasn't the most comfortable position, but the bonds on her wrists were loose enough that it wasn't so bad. She could even get out if she wanted to.

But she kept thinking about that poor little girl. She

wanted to help her—needed to help her. So she'd wait. And hope.

Hazeleigh had no idea how much time had passed when she heard the distant rumble of an engine. She didn't think it was big enough to be a truck, which was too bad because that would have meant Cal and Dunne were here to save her and tell her everything was fine.

Instead, this sounded more like some kind of four-wheeler or small utility vehicle. It got closer and closer, and then came to a stop not far from her. A light clicked on and Hazeleigh had to flinch against the sudden brightness against her eyes—headlights from the small vehicle.

"Well, well, well, you don't disappoint," a man's voice said.

Hazeleigh managed to blink her eyes open. The light was still too bright and shining directly at her so she couldn't see him, but she could make out the little girl to the side.

"But where's…?" The girl frowned in confusion, but the man didn't express any dismay at there only being one person tied to a tree.

So Hazeleigh maintained eye contact with the little girl. "Thank God you're back. I hate being left all alone in the dark."

The girl frowned but said nothing else. The man finally stepped out from the bright light so she could see him. Tall, broad. Older than her, definitely, but the heavy beard made it hard to discern a real age even with the flecks of gray. Dark eyes, thick eyebrows, and all together it made Hazeleigh realize something that made her stomach sink.

He looked like Mr. Field. There were differences, and maybe she was looking so hard for *some* understanding that she was making things up. But she'd spent the last seven years spending a lot of time with the man, and they looked very similar.

"Who are you?" Hazeleigh asked.

"You don't recognize me? That hurts my feelings." He did not in any way sound like his feelings were hurt. "Of course, you and your obnoxious sister were always too good to pay much attention to the help, weren't you?"

The acidic words didn't make sense to Hazeleigh. Dad had never hired on much help. Except… "The only *help* we had was when my mother was *dying.*"

"Oh, boo-hoo. Zara was out working while you and the other one were living the high life."

The high life? Watching her mother wither away at *nine.* But if he was working at the ranch, surely… "So… you're a Chinelly." Not a Field?

"Don't put that on me. Hamilton might be my mother's brother, but that doesn't make me a Chinelly. Good blood blots out the bad. Right, Sarabeth?" He gave the girl's hair a rough tousle and she winced. "Maybe my blood will win inside you yet."

Sarabeth didn't respond. She looked at the ground. Hazeleigh's heart ached for her.

"Are you going to let my mother go now?" she asked him. But she already sounded defeated, like she wasn't sure he would.

The man laughed, the sound dark and mean. "Sure. We'll just let you both run off. I was wrong—you are as dumb as your mother." He gave her a rough shove, knocking her down.

Hazeleigh made a move to step forward and help the girl, but the ties on her wrists and the leash stopped her.

"All right. Let's get you somewhere we can really talk." He moved to the tree and untied the leash but didn't untie the wire around her hands. "God, Sarabeth. Learn how to tie a damn knot, huh?" He tightened them with one rough jerk then dragged Hazeleigh to the utility vehicle. He shoved her into the passenger seat and then hopped into the driver's seat…leaving Sarabeth sitting in the grass.

"What about your daughter?"

The man threw back his head and laughed.

Hazeleigh could only watch over her shoulder as the man drove them away, the girl disappearing into the dark.

LANDON FOUND ZARA and Jake first, though he was out of breath with a cramp in his side that felt like fire. His skin burned everywhere the fire of the explosion had hit, but he did his best to hide that. Ignore it. He explained everything that had happened, and they relayed their end of things. They'd been closing the circle, but no one had been found out yet. No signs of life. So none of the mysterious "they" had rounded them up.

"This just gets weirder and weirder," Landon muttered. "Look, if you guys haven't found signs of anything, they have to be at the house in the center. Let's walkie everyone. Meet at that spot on the map Cal and Dunne were supposed to stop at with the truck."

The walkies crackled in the quiet dark, but everyone agreed to meet. Jake got off his horse and gave it to Landon, and then got on the back of Zara's with her. With no words spoken, they took off—closer to the supposed house, closer to the center of everything.

It had to be the center of everything, because if it wasn't...

Landon didn't let himself think of the bad possibilities. He could only think of finding answers. Only the mission.

He was a soldier now. Nothing else.

He wasn't sure how long it took them to all convene at the spot behind a swell of land. They were still quite a way from the house, but there was a little light visible now. Someone was definitely down there in the valley.

"Well, this is a mess, isn't it?" Henry muttered.

"Always so positive," Zara replied.

Landon ignored them both. He had a plan. It wasn't perfect, but it was fast, and with Hazeleigh tied up alone somewhere out there, he figured it had to be.

"We stick in teams of two, except Cal will go with me and Dunne will stay with the truck. Things get bad, he can call the cops and we'll deal with that fallout later. The rest of us will circle, moving forward until we have a better idea of what's going on in there. They have someone, this little girl's mother. They're after Hazeleigh for information. They've killed before."

Landon waited for someone to argue with his plan, but no one did. The silence of the night settled around them. Agreement.

He blew out a breath, ready to give the order to move

forward. But the echo of running horse hooves had them all turning. His brothers had their guns drawn. Landon hoped against hope it was Hazeleigh.

He flipped on his flashlight, trusting his brothers to know what to do if it was someone here to hurt them.

He recognized Buttercup first, but it wasn't Hazeleigh on her. "Stand down," he said in a low voice to his brothers, still holding their guns. "It's the little girl."

"You mean the one who shot at you?" Henry replied dryly.

"Hell, Landon, you're burned," Jake rasped now that he could see in the light.

"Nothing serious."

"Nothing serious? You have to—"

"End this. First and foremost. We have to end this."

The girl pulled the horse to a halt in front of them. "He has your friend. I know where she is. If you promise to get my mother out when you get her out, I'll help you."

"How can you help?" Henry demanded.

The girl rolled her eyes. "Because I know everything, duh."

"Tell us who *he* is," Landon demanded.

"My father. Rob Currington."

"Currington. He was a ranch hand for us when I was a kid," Zara said. "With Hamilton Chinelly."

"Hamilton's a pawn in all this. Everyone's a pawn. That's what he always says, anyway," the girl said. "We have to hurry. He wants this over tonight. He promised me if I gave him the lady, he'd let me and my mother go. But he lied. He's going to kill everyone once he gets what he wants. I'm not going to let him kill my mother."

And I'm not going to let him kill Hazeleigh.

"What does he want?" Cal had the presence of mind to ask the question, when all Landon could think of was retribution.

"He found some of the bank-robbery gold, but some of it's still missing. She's the only one who knows where it is now that he killed his father."

Mr. Field. It still wasn't making a ton of sense, but it sure all connected a little clearer.

"She's in the house?"

"He has my mother chained up in the basement with one of his cousins watching her. I think that's where he'll take Hazeleigh. But you have to be careful. The house is falling down. You can't just run in. You have to follow me."

Landon could tell that his brothers didn't like that idea, but he didn't see as they had much of a choice. "All right."

The girl swung down from the horse. She didn't have her guns anymore, but when she stepped into the small circle of light Landon's flashlight made, he could see her nose was bleeding.

"I'll do everything I can to get your mother out," he promised, wanting to give her shoulder a reassuring squeeze. She shifted away, the movement sharp enough that he had the sneaking suspicion she also knew what it felt like to have her father rough her up.

"You'll follow me. You'll listen to me. Or we're all dead." She was so serious. So fierce. Landon didn't want to think of what had made a girl of ten that hardened.

"Looks like we've got ourselves a mini Cal," Henry said. "Lead the way, kid."

They set out, six full-grown military men and one ranch woman, following a little girl into danger.

Chapter Twenty-Three

The house was in ruins. The man dragged Hazeleigh out of the utility vehicle and toward it, like they were going to go inside, when she couldn't imagine the house being able to stand the weight of much of anything. The roof was caved in at spots, the walls had buckled in others.

But he walked straight for the front door and kicked it open, dragging her behind.

"Be careful now. One wrong step and *whoops* you'll find yourself bloody and broken, nine feet down onto the hard concrete below."

Hazeleigh swallowed. She eyed the floor. All was dark except there was a little beam of light coming up from the floorboards. She believed him. If the floor had this many cracks that it showed off the light below, she might crash right through.

He led her through the house, and she could tell that he was being very careful of where they stepped. This house was definitely not safe to be in. She hoped Landon and everyone would recognize that before they came in guns blazing.

Because they would come. They would save her. It

would all be okay. She had to believe that. It was the only way to get through this.

He finally made it to a cellar-type entrance in the back of the house, though whatever door had once been there was long gone. He pulled her down rickety stairs, now much less careful about where and how they stepped.

In the basement, lamps were lit. One man stood there, beefy arms crossed, many guns strapped to his person. A woman sat in a corner, tied to a chair.

Hazeleigh didn't recognize either of them. But the woman's face made her gut churn with anxiety. She was severely bruised, with dried blood coming from her nose and mouth and ear. She didn't even look up when they entered the room.

"Sarabeth came through, huh?" the man said, sounding surprised.

"That she did. Get another chair and some zip ties."

The man rushed to do as he was told and pulled an old metal folding chair to the center of the room. "Gonna let Jessie go, then?"

The man let out a nasty laugh. "Like hell. Once we have what we need, everyone is going up in flames. *Everyone.* And no one will ever know I was here."

The man roughly grabbed Hazeleigh and tied her to the metal chair. She didn't fight him. There didn't seem much point. Even if she could get away from them, she couldn't run upstairs. She'd just fall right through.

Besides, Landon knew she was here. He'd figure it out. She was trusting him to do what needed to be done, all so they could help save that little girl.

Please be okay, Sarabeth.

"Now, where's the rest of it?"

She looked at the man, who looked so much like a young Mr. Field it was disorienting. "I don't know what you're talking about."

The backhanded slap was so sudden, she hadn't even flinched before the pain exploded across her cheek. She nearly toppled to the side, chair and all, but the other man must have grabbed the chair, and she was yanked back with a jarring thud.

"I want to know where the rest of the gold is. It was supposed to be in that stupid schoolhouse, but there was only a quarter of it. That dumb old man kept babbling about a lot more than what we got."

So it was true. "You killed Mr. Field over some fake gold?"

"Fake? Fake." He stormed over to a duffel bag and undid the zipper, tipping it so she could see inside. Coins jangled together. "This isn't fake." He stormed back over to her. "Where's the rest of it?"

"I don't—" The slap was on the opposite side this time. Her skin was on fire. She felt rattled and tears formed in her eyes—from both emotion and pure pain.

"He told you everything. You organized *everything*. That stupid old man told me that if there was something to know his assistant *knew* it. Begged me to let him live so he could call you. He was my father and he trusted *you*."

"Your father? You killed your father?" Mr. Field had a son he'd never told anyone about.

"He was never a father to me. Paid off my mother, sent her away, all so he could look for gold. Well, I found the damn gold, didn't I? But there's supposed to be more, and I want it."

It was more than greed. Something twisted up in his relationship, or lack of one, with his father. "I didn't know everything, because I didn't know about you."

That seemed to stop him for a second. But only a second. Another blow landed and this time she couldn't hold back the sob of pain. She understood why the other woman in the room just sat there, unmoving. There was nothing to do but absorb the pain and hope—hope that help would come.

LANDON CAME TO a stop when the little girl leading them did. They stood just off the porch that was now little more than splintered boards and rubble.

"The floor inside isn't stable," she whispered. "They've been hiding in the basement, and there's only one way to get down there. You have to be careful."

"You're sure there's only two men in there?" Cal asked in a low tone.

"There only have been this whole time. Hamilton would come sometimes, but he was too scared to go in. Dad's cousin, Ben, almost never leaves. Dad comes and goes."

"He lets you come and go?" Landon asked gently.

"He doesn't care what I do as long as I keep out of his way and do what he asks right when he asks."

"Okay. So what do we call you?"

"Bigfo—"

"What's your name?" Landon said, firmly but gently.

"Sarabeth," she muttered. "If you don't get my mom out, I am going to kill you. I swear it."

"I believe you." And he did. Maybe he wouldn't *let* her kill him, but he had no doubt she would try. "You're a brave one, Sarabeth. Your mom's going to be very proud when we get her out of there. But you're going to have to—"

"I have to lead you. If you don't follow me in, you'll fall through the floor. Even if not, he's going to hear you and start shooting." She sucked in a deep breath. "The less people that go in there, the better chance we have of making it through."

"A shooting gauntlet. Fun," Henry said.

"No." Landon straightened, eyeing the house. "If just Sarabeth and I go in, we might be able to avoid being heard. Or if he thinks it's just her, we might not get shot at. You guys can wait out here—"

"Landon—"

"No, hear me out, Cal. Someone starts shooting, you can all rush in. But if we can sneak in, element of surprise works in our favor. Two guys? I can take out two guys. You know I can."

"Even all burnt up like that?"

"I'm fine," Landon insisted. "Sarabeth and I go in and see what we can do. You guys are backup. Deal?"

There was a gradual assent, though no one seemed too happy about it. But they didn't have time for options everyone loved.

"All right, Sarabeth."

"You're going to need this." She shrugged off her backpack and then held out his gun, which she'd made him put down back at the schoolhouse.

Landon took it and put it back in its holster. "Thanks. You still got yours?"

She pulled it out. "Yeah."

"Can you aim?"

"Missed you on purpose earlier."

He didn't know if it was true or if she was trying to make herself feel better, but hopefully they got out of this without her needing to shoot.

"Go on, then. Lead the way."

She crept over the rubble of the porch, barely making a sound. Landon did his best to copy her every move. She got to the door, paused and then pushed it open slowly—so slowly, no noise was made.

She slid into the opening she'd made. Not big enough for him, but he copied her, moving the door with minuscule pressure so as not to make a sound.

He heard the low rumble of voices and then a *thwack*. The sound of flesh hitting flesh, and the muted whimper of a woman.

He might have leaped forward, but Sarabeth put her hand on his. Her little fingers curled around his hand, and she led him forward. Inch by inch.

He followed her steps exactly, but something rattled next to them—probably a mouse, and Sarabeth jumped and stumbled a little bit, making enough noise with splintering wood to attract attention.

Landon reached out and grabbed her as her ankle went through the floor. He steadied her back on the good part of the floor, but someone would be coming. He lowered his free hand to his gun.

"Rob?" Sarabeth called out. "It's me. I'm okay."

"Damn it," someone rumbled from below. "She really is a cockroach. Get your butt down here, then."

Landon let out the quietest breath he could manage.

She might have stumbled, but she'd just saved the day. No one seemed to suspect she might be with someone.

She started moving forward again, slower this time. Landon followed, trying to make his foot land at the same time hers did so it didn't sound like two pairs of footsteps, but it was too risky to keep going that way.

He reached out, stopped Sarabeth's progress. "Let me pick you up," he said, barely disturbing the air he'd spoken the words so quietly. He didn't wait for assent. She stiffened as he put his hands on her waist, but let him lift her off the ground. "One set of footsteps," he said into her ear.

He felt her nod against him. Then he moved forward the last few steps in the line they'd been following. There was an opening, light shining through. He set her down at the top of the stairs.

She looked back at him, held up her hands. Ten fingers.

Ten seconds.

He nodded. She scrambled down the stairs, making a ruckus as she did. Landon could hear the grumbles, but thankfully there were no more blows.

He counted in his head. Ten seconds. He didn't know what she planned to do with ten seconds, but he trusted her. He had to trust her.

Once he hit ten, he snuck down the stairs. He ducked into the basement just in time to see Sarabeth go flying, her gun clattering out of her grasp and her head hitting the concrete hard and going still—far too still. Hazeleigh let out a gasp of pain—her face was red and bruised. Another woman, bloody and bruised, was tied up in the corner.

In the span of only seconds, Landon was across the room—one hand grabbing the gun moving toward him and his other a fist going into the shorter man's neck.

The gun clattered to the ground, and the man who'd been throat-punched choked out a gurgled gasp.

Then it was a melee. Punches, kicks. He dodged blows, landed them. Two against one, but he'd beaten these odds before, and he wasn't about to let either man lay another hand on any of the women they'd abused.

The shorter guy managed to get an arm around Landon's neck, but that gave Landon the leverage to flip him over. He knew it left him vulnerable to the other man, but if he could take out this one—

He stepped on his throat, the man struggling but fading fast. When he looked behind him, he saw it was a mistake. The other man had grabbed his gun and was moving it in Landon's direction.

The gun went off—an echoing boom in the basement—but not *that* gun. The man—this Rob Currington—jerked once, the gun sliding from his grasp as he fell to the floor. Lifeless.

Landon whirled toward the new shooter who'd just essentially saved his life.

But it wasn't one of his brothers.

It was Sarabeth.

Chapter Twenty-Four

She didn't fall apart. After a few moments, Sarabeth carefully put down the gun and went and untied her mother's bonds, which spurred Landon into action, and he'd come to untie Hazeleigh.

"You're hurt," he murmured, gently undoing the ties.

"I'm alive." Hazeleigh turned to look at the little girl trying to help her mother to stand as the cavalry rushed in. The Thompson brothers. Zara.

Zara made a beeline for Hazeleigh.

"Everyone's okay," Landon assured her, helping her to her feet.

"Oh, Landon, you're burnt." His shirt was torn and the nasty blisters... It must have happened in the explosion, and he hadn't let on all this time.

"And your face looks like it was used as a punching bag," Zara said flatly.

"He thought I knew where this other gold is, but I don't."

"Other gold?"

Hazeleigh pointed to the bag. "He found some of the bank-robbery gold."

There was a moment of silence. "Mr. Field was… right," Zara said.

Emotion clogged Hazeleigh's throat. Poor Mr. Field. All that work. All that time. And it had been there. He'd never get the chance to see it.

"He found out that old guy was his father, and thought he'd know where the gold was," Sarabeth said.

"Since I'm connected to the Petersons," the mother said, leaning on Henry, who'd helped Sarabeth get her out of the chair. Her eye was swollen shut and her voice was weak, but she seemed determined to explain. "This land where Mr. Field thought the gold was—Rob came and got me from where I'd been hiding Sarabeth from him."

"You pretended to be hurt," Landon said, crouching down to study Sarabeth's face. "When your dad threw you, you pretended to be hurt." He sounded amazed.

Sarabeth looked toward her father's body, but the Thompsons had made themselves into a kind of shield so neither the body nor the blood could be seen. She shrugged. "Yeah, figured you could use some help."

Landon kneeled in front of her. He reached out but dropped his hands before he touched her. "Thank you," he said sincerely.

"Yeah, well. Thanks to you, too, I guess. You helped. I couldn't do it myself." She leaned into her mother, who seemed shaky at best. "I couldn't get her out my-self."

"But you helped," Hazeleigh said, her voice sounding raw even to her. Her face throbbed, but every-thing was…

Well, not okay. People were dead. But answers had been found.

Even when the police came, thanks to Dunne calling them in, Sarabeth didn't fall apart. She held her mother's hand, and let Hazeleigh hold her other, and she told the cops everything.

From her father kidnapping them from their house in Arizona, to what Rob had told her about Mr. Field and the gold over the course of the last few weeks, down to her shooting her own father to save Landon.

Hazeleigh was no longer a person of interest, and the man who'd killed Mr. Field was no longer a threat.

The ambulance took away the body of Rob Currington and the wounded cousin, the Thompson brothers once again making sure Sarabeth didn't see the body. When the EMTs came, they insisted that Landon, Hazeleigh, Sarabeth and her mother, Jessie, go to the hospital.

The rest got a little fuzzy. By the time Hazeleigh was home again, with painkillers and ice packs but luckily no broken bones, she hardly remembered the trip. But Zara bundled her inside, tucked her into her old room in the main house and Hazeleigh slept for what felt like days.

When she woke up, she was disoriented for a moment. Because it was her old, childhood room, but the bed was bigger and the decor was different.

And there was a man in it. Snoring softly.

She looked over at him, her heart swelling painfully. They'd survived. Figured it out. He'd been by her side, he'd trusted her, and in the end he hadn't just saved her, he'd made sure to save that little girl. Who'd been brave enough to save them both.

His eyes blinked open as if he could sense her looking at him even in a deep sleep. He shifted. "You're up," he rasped.

"I am." She looked around the room. It looked like daytime, but she didn't have the foggiest idea when she'd gone to sleep. "I don't know what day it is, but I am up."

"Wednesday," he said with a yawn. He glanced at the clock. "I think."

Then he carefully wrapped his arm around her, and she snuggled in. Relief. "Everything is going to be okay."

"Yeah, it is." She was tempted to fall back asleep. "Sarabeth?"

"Her and her mother are with family services figuring everything out. They're in good hands, and they'll be okay. We'll make sure of it."

We'll make sure of it. Hazeleigh smiled and sank into him again, relaxing. Sarabeth and her mother might not know it yet, but they'd just joined their cobbled-together family. "Really good." She sighed heavily. "She saved us. Well, you both saved us and—"

"I think we worked together to save each other," he interrupted. "A team."

"A family," Hazeleigh corrected.

He chuckled, though it seemed a little sad, and he stiffened underneath her cheek. "Speaking of family… Look…" He cleared his throat. "There's more than just the military thing you should know, Hazeleigh. Now that everything is going to calm down… The thing is, the six of us were in the military together. But we're not actual biological brothers. Because of a military mistake, we had to have our identities wiped and disappear. Start this new…fake, quiet life."

"I guess Wilde seemed like a good place for a quiet life on paper."

"Seemed like indeed." He chuckled, then winced a little. But he kept her hand in his, as if inspecting her fingers. "I'm sorry if that feels like a lie."

"Did you lie?" It didn't feel like a lie. An omission maybe, but nothing…horrible. Nothing that changed how she felt about them.

"I'm not related to them. My last name isn't Thompson. These are lies."

Hazeleigh rolled to face him, studying all that guilt. So serious. So frustrated with himself. She understood it well. She understood *him* well. And she was pretty confident they'd grow to understand each other even better. In all that love they had for one another.

"But they're your brothers, blood or not. They're your family, even if you chose the name Thompson rather than having it handed to you at birth. And you're telling me now, when it's important. I'm not going to hold it against you, Landon. And I'm not going to let you be a martyr about it."

"I guess we're pretty good at that—not letting each other martyr ourselves." He smiled and touched her cheek.

"Yeah, we are. I think we're going to be pretty good at loving each other."

"Yeah, I think we are."

In that moment she realized she didn't *think* they were going to be good at it.

She knew.

* * * * *

COMING NEXT MONTH FROM

◆HARLEQUIN

INTRIGUE

#2133 SET UP IN THE CITY
A Colt Brothers Investigation • by B.J. Daniels
All hell breaks loose when Willie Colt's extradited felon disappears. He knows he was set up, and he'll need big-city attorney Ellie Shaffer to prove it. But nothing—and no one—is what it seems. Soon the dangerous truth about their connection to the criminal is revealed...

#2134 RESCUED BY THE RANCHER
The Cowboys of Cider Creek • by Barb Han
When rancher Callum Hayes opens his home to Payton Reinert, he knows she's the only woman who escaped the Masked Monster alive. But how far will Callum go to protect her from a deranged killer determined that she won't escape a second time?

#2135 SHOT IN THE DARK
Covert Cowboy Soldiers • by Nicole Helm
Hardened ex-marine Henry Thompson is no babysitter. But when Jessie Peterson begs for his help locating her rebellious daughter, his military-rescue instincts kick in. Family treasure, secret doppelgängers and dogged gunfire are no match for Henry's guard. Jessie, however, is another story...

#2136 TEXAS BODYGUARD: BRAX
San Antonio Security • by Janie Crouch
When security specialist Brax Patterson gains custody of his nephew, nanny Tessa Mahoney is a godsend. But his beautiful, secretive employee is more than she seems...and brings danger to Brax's front door. Is Tessa an innocent victim of the cartel he's investigating or the one pulling all the strings?

#2137 CATCHING THE CARLING LAKE KILLER
West Investigations • by K.D. Richards
Journalist Simone Jarrett is haunted by the murder she witnessed years ago. But instead of closure, her return to Carling Lake brings her Sheriff Lance Webb. With the body count climbing, Lance fears the Card Killer is back to terrorize the woman who got away.

#2138 RESOLUTE AIM
The Protectors of Boone County, Texas • by Leslie Marshman
Deputy Noah Reed has always been a risk-taker—the exact opposite of his trigger-shy new partner. But Bree Delgado is no green cop. With a meth ring exposed and drug runners out for revenge, the bad boy out to make good will have to trust her to protect his back...and his heart.

YOU CAN FIND MORE INFORMATION ON UPCOMING HARLEQUIN TITLES, FREE EXCERPTS AND MORE AT HARLEQUIN.COM.

HICNM0223

HARLEQUIN
PLUS

Try the best multimedia
subscription service for romance
readers like you!

Read, Watch and Play.

Experience the easiest way to get
the romance content you crave.

Start your **FREE TRIAL** at
www.harlequinplus.com/freetrial.